When the noi
earthquake
spoke, his voi
as he assumed leadership.

'Come on,' he urged, 'let's go outside.'

They had only just begun to move when there came another earth-shattering roar, much louder this time, and as the building shook and shuddered again wooden rafters and great chunks of masonry came crashing down in front of them.

As Claire screamed Dominic pulled her into his arms and, throwing her to the floor, shielded her with his body as hell itself seemed to unleash around them and stone, wood and plaster crashed to the ground…

Laura MacDonald lives in the Isle of Wight and is married with a grown-up family. She has enjoyed writing fiction since she was a child and for several years has worked for members of the medical profession, both in pharmacy and in general practice. Her daughter is a nurse and has helped with the research for Laura's medical stories.

Recent titles by the same author:

UNDER SPECIAL CARE
POLICE DOCTOR
MEDIC ON APPROVAL
THE SURGEON'S DILEMMA
A VERY TENDER PRACTICE
DR PRESTON'S DAUGHTER

MEDITERRANEAN RESCUE

BY
LAURA MACDONALD

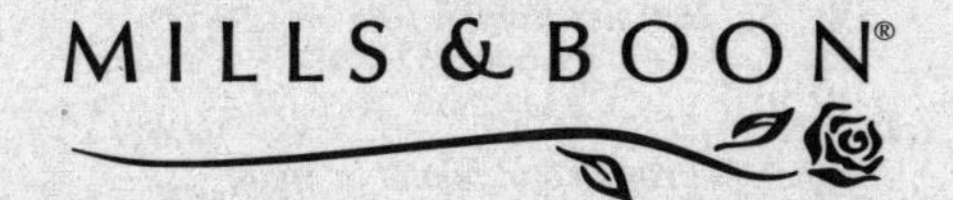

First published in Great Britain 2003
Harlequin Mills & Boon Limited,
Eton House, 18-24 Paradise Road, Richmond, Surrey TW9 1SR

ISBN 0 263 83464 6

Set in Times Roman 10½ on 11½ pt.
03-0803-52189

Printed and bound in Spain
by Litografia Rosés, S.A., Barcelona

CHAPTER ONE

'YOU need to throw another, you know.'

'I'm sorry?' Shielding her eyes from the hot Italian sun, Claire looked up into the face of the man who stood at her side.

'A coin in the fountain,' he explained. 'You've thrown your one for luck but you need to throw another to ensure your return to Rome.'

'Really?' Claire peered down into the clear green water to where her coin was indistinguishable from the many others that lay on the bottom.

'Absolutely,' he said firmly, then, as she glanced up at him again, he added, 'Always assuming, of course, that you would want to return.'

'Oh, yes,' she said quickly, 'yes, of course. Who wouldn't?' she added.

'Yes, quite.' The man lowered himself to sit beside her on the stone wall surrounding the magnificent Trevi fountain. 'Although, I suppose,' he went on after a moment, 'there might well be some who would have had their fill the first time of ancient buildings, monuments and churches, to say nothing of the insanity of the drivers and the price of a cup of coffee.'

'Oh, I think I could overlook those things,' Claire replied lightly. 'As far as I'm concerned, they are more than compensated for by others—the splendour of it all...' She waved one slender hand in the direction of the gushing water as it poured from the open mouths of stone gargoyles. 'The atmosphere, the sunshine... Oh, and the ice cream—

that's just out of this world and I don't care how much it costs.'

'In that case, I would say a second coin is essential,' he replied solemnly.

'Right.' Standing up, Claire unzipped her shoulder-bag, which she wore across her body, having been warned about pickpockets, rummaged inside, opened her purse and took out a coin. 'I'd better do this properly,' she said. Turning so that she stood with her back to the fountain, she threw the coin over her shoulder into the water where it joined the hundreds of others. 'There,' she said, looking down at the man, 'that's done. But what about you?' she added on a sudden impulse.

'What about me?' He raised eyebrows as dark as his hair, and his eyes widened. They were very expressive eyes, she noticed, brown and with a depth of intensity in their gaze that seemed to suggest he could read her thoughts. The idea threw her slightly and she found herself averting her gaze as she pursued her question.

'Well, have you thrown your coin or coins? Or maybe you have so much luck in your life already you do not feel in need of more, and perhaps the noise and the traffic has got to you so much you have no desire to return?'

She saw his features relax slightly into the semblance of a smile. 'Not at all,' he said. He stood up. 'I threw my coins, both of them, before you came along.'

'Ah,' she said, 'so you, too, wish to return.'

'Of course,' he said. 'Like you say, who wouldn't?' He paused and, turning, lifted his head and took a deep breath as if inhaling the very essence of Rome. Claire noticed that his hair, which at first had appeared straight, had a rather disconcerting tendency to curl at the nape of his neck. She wasn't sure why she should find it disconcerting but it somehow made him appear vulnerable. He wore a dark blue T-shirt and faded denims and Claire was aware of powerful muscles that rippled across his shoulders. He remained silent after that and Claire didn't really know what else to say. She wasn't in the habit of speaking to strangers, even English ones in a foreign country, although strictly speaking he wasn't a complete stranger.

Reinforcing her theory that he might be able to read her thoughts, he suddenly spoke again. 'I believe,' he said, 'we are staying at the same hotel.'

'Yes,' she agreed, 'I believe we are.' She spoke lightly, casually as if it was of little consequence, but she had seen him at the hotel, of course she had. In the foyer the first time she couldn't have failed to notice him for together with his dark classical good looks he stood several inches above everyone else. Their eyes had met, their gazes holding for a fraction longer than was deemed seemly before looking quickly away. Then they had both then looked again as if each had recognised the other only to realise they hadn't known each other, and in the brief ensuing moment of confusion to look away for the second time. And after that, she had been only too aware of him—in the hotel dining room or foyer. And yesterday, on the guided tour that had been arranged by the hotel, she had been only too conscious of his presence as together with a dozen or so other English guests they had dutifully trailed behind their Italian guide as he had conducted them around St Peter's and parts of the Vatican state.

Today she hadn't seen him at breakfast and she had left the hotel early and alone to browse at her own pace suddenly very conscious and somewhat down-hearted that she *was* alone in this beautiful and most romantic of cities. She was only too aware that he was the sort of man she would once have been deeply attracted to just as she also knew that he had been attracted to her, and where once she might have been pleased at the prospect, might have welcomed it, pursued it, even if it might have led only to a holiday romance—there was no question of that for now there was another consideration in her life.

'Through there…' he suddenly lifted one hand, indicating a road facing the fountain '…there's a nice little street café. Do you fancy joining me for a cappuccino?'

She shouldn't, she knew that, just as she knew this attraction between herself and this stranger was definitely not something to be pursued or encouraged. It was something to be nipped in the bud before it had a chance to even start.

'I'd love to,' she heard herself say.

The café was on one corner of a sun-drenched piazza and they found a table beneath a green-and-white-striped umbrella in the shade of a plane tree.

'It seems hotter than ever today,' said Claire, after a waiter had taken their order and disappeared inside the café.

'It is,' her companion agreed. 'In fact, it feels like we could be in for a storm.'

'Do you think so?' Claire frowned and peered up at the sky, lifting her sunglasses to gauge the depth of its colour. 'I can't see any stormclouds and the sky is as blue as it could possibly be.'

'It's just something in the atmosphere.' He lifted his shoulders in a slight shrug. 'But let's not worry about it for now. I would say if we are to have a storm it's some way off.' He paused and, leaning back in his chair, tilted his head to one side and looked keenly at her. In that moment it was as if he took in every detail of her appearance, from her long honey-blonde hair and hazel eyes to her creamy skin already touched by the sun. 'I think it's time we introduced ourselves,' he said at last. 'I'm Dominic Hansford.' Leaning forward again, he held out his right hand, half-rising out of his chair.

'Claire Schofield.' His outstretched hand took hers in a firm grip that was surprisingly cool given the heat of the day.

'So what brings you to Rome?' he asked as he resumed his seat.

'It's somewhere I've always meant to visit,' she replied, 'but somehow never got around to.' She paused. 'What about you?'

'The same really.' He nodded. 'The thing is, I've travelled all over the world but I never really got to see Europe so I'm trying to remedy that now. You're travelling alone.' It was more of a statement of the obvious than a question, but he nevertheless raised his dark eyebrows.

'Yes,' she said. 'I was due to come with somebody but they had to cry off at the last minute so rather than waste the ticket I decided to come alone. How about you?' she added almost as an afterthought.

'Oh, I invariably travel alone.' He turned, swivelling in his chair as the waiter arrived bearing a tray with two steaming cups of cappuccino. Claire found herself studying him afresh—the chiselled features, the firm line of his jaw and the way his eyes crinkled at the corners when he smiled. When he glanced back at her after the waiter had departed, she hurriedly looked away. 'I find I get to see more that way,' he added.

'You say you've travelled a lot—where exactly?' Suddenly she was intensely curious to know just where his travels had taken him and why.

'Oh, Thailand, Afghanistan, India,' he said, 'and more recently South America—Chile and Peru.'

'Sounds wonderful,' she replied with a little sigh as gently she stirred her cappuccino, watching the swirls of chocolate settle into the froth.

'It was,' he agreed, 'or at least parts of it were. Sometimes it was pretty gruelling.'

'So was this business or pleasure?' She took a sip of her drink, licking the froth from her top lip with the tip of her tongue.

'Mainly work, I'm afraid.' Lifting his own cup, he took a mouthful.

'I rather thought it might be.' She nodded. 'So what is it that you do?'

Dominic didn't answer immediately and Claire got the impression he was almost reluctant to reply. Then, after carefully placing his cup back in its saucer, he said, 'I'm a doctor.'

For some reason she wasn't surprised. There was something about him that suggested both the sensitivity and the strength of character necessary to be a doctor. What did surprise her, however, was the extent of his foreign travel, which seemed to have little in common with the GPs of her acquaintance. 'So how come you get to travel so much?' she asked. 'Most doctors I know don't seem to go much farther than the annual family camping trip to the South of France.'

'Know many doctors, do you?' There was amusement in the dark eyes now.

'Probably more than most,' she replied, then, aware of his quick, curious glance, added, 'I'm a nurse.'

'Ah,' he said, and the single word seemed to confirm some preconceived theory of his. 'I felt we had something in common.' He paused, took another mouthful of his coffee then, leaning back in his chair again, said, 'So where do you nurse?'

'In a large group practice near Guildford in Surrey, it's called the Hargreaves Centre—you may have heard of it.'

He nodded. 'Yes, I believe I have—wasn't it founded by Hargreaves of fertility treatment fame?'

'Yes,' she replied, 'Charles Hargreaves. He was father of Richard Hargreaves, who is the present senior partner of the practice.'

'How long have you been there?'

'Only a couple of years. Before that I was in hospital work—mainly psychiatric and rehabilitation.'

'Are you happy in general practice?'

'Yes, reasonably.' She considered for a moment. 'I assist in general clinics but I've also been taking part recently in stress-management counselling.' She paused. 'It's unbelievable how many conditions arise from stress and anxiety,' she added.

'I can imagine.' He nodded. 'A friend of mine has recently had to give up practice entirely because of a stress-related condition.'

'We are having to find a locum for one of our partners who is being forced to take a sabbatical because he is completely stressed out.' Claire paused then, aware of the heat of the sun, which was beginning to burn her shoulders around the thin straps of the white sundress she wore, stood up and eased her chair further into the shade. 'So what is your field?' she asked as she sat down again.

'I've been working with various charities,' he replied, 'mainly children's charities—Save the Children, Médecins Sans Frontières, Voluntary Service Overseas, that sort of thing.'

'Do you mean in war zones?' she asked curiously.

'Sometimes, yes. We go in as a team after some conflict or sometimes after a disaster or famine. Whatever it is, there are always children caught up in it.' He sighed. 'It is our job to treat their medical needs and at the same time, if it is at all possible, to bring back some semblance of normality into their shattered lives.'

'It must be rewarding work,' she said slowly.

'In some instances, yes, it is,' he agreed, 'but at other times you have to guard against being totally overwhelmed by the sheer magnitude of what is being attempted. We have to remember that many of the children we treat may have been orphaned and may have lost siblings and other members of their families, some have been badly injured or maimed and others are desperately sick with little hope of recovery.'

'So are you between assignments at the moment?'

'My last posting was in South America, where we were coping with the aftermath of flooding,' he replied.

'And I suppose next you wait to see where you are needed?'

'Actually I've been taking a break from overseas work,' he admitted. 'After South America I returned to Warwickshire because my father is ill. I have been doing temporary locum work at the local hospital in Accident and Emergency.'

'Any plans to return abroad?' she asked with interest.

'Eventually, but not immediately.' Dominic appeared to consider. 'I'm enjoying the slower pace of life,' he went on after a moment, 'and it's been nice to be able to spend a bit of time with my father.'

'And now you're in Rome on holiday.'

'Yes,' he agreed, lifting his face to the sun, 'now I'm in Rome.'

Claire remained silent, considering all he had told her. His work sounded fascinating and she longed to know more, but a glance at his face revealed that his eyes were closed and somehow she felt unable to question him further, as if by closing his eyes he was dissuading any further conversation about his work.

They sat in companionable silence while the bustle of the busy piazza went on around them. Just as Claire was wondering what to say next, it was Dominic who broke the silence. 'Are you going on this excursion tomorrow?' he asked.

'What excursion?' She frowned.

'To Assisi,' he replied, 'and apparently stopping at a village and a monastery *en route* whose names escape me.'

'I haven't heard anything about that,' said Claire.

'The rep came into the dining room after breakfast and announced it,' he went on. 'I think you may have already left.'

'I must have done,' she replied, 'I certainly don't know anything about it.'

'Well, I'm sure it won't be too late to put your name down when we get back,' he said, 'always supposing, of course, that you want to go.'

'Yes, I would like to go,' said Claire slowly. 'I've always wanted to visit Assisi. Was there much interest?'

He nodded. 'Yes, I got the impression most of the other guests wanted to go.' Pushing his chair back, he stood up. 'Look,' he said, 'why don't we wander back now and see if we can put your name down?'

'All right.' Claire also rose to her feet, picking up her bag and slipping the strap over her head again before taking out her purse to pay for her coffee.

'Please,' said Dominic, 'let me get these.'

'Thank you,' said Claire a moment later as he joined her on the pavement after settling the bill.

'Don't mention it.' He smiled. He had a lovely smile, revealing even, very white teeth.

Together they made their way through the maze of narrow streets to the hotel where Claire found she was able to add her name to the list for the following day's excursion.

'What are you going to do now?' asked Dominic as she turned away from the hotel's reception desk.

'Oh, I think a quick dip in the pool, lunch, then a siesta,' Claire replied, wondering even as she spoke what she would say if he asked if she would join him for lunch. She needn't have worried, however, for at that moment they were joined by two other English guests who were staying at the hotel and whose acquaintance Claire had already made.

'Oh, Claire, there you are,' said the woman. 'We've been looking for you.' Melanie Frazer, dark-haired, vivacious and trendy, was a fashion buyer for a well-known high-street chain store and was touring Italy with her partner, Peter Hamilton, a quantity surveyor. 'We thought you would probably want to go on the Assisi trip,' Melanie went on, 'but we weren't sure so we didn't put your name down.'

'Well, I've done it now,' said Claire.

'Will you join us for lunch?' Melanie went on enthusiastically. 'We're meeting up with Ted and May on the Renaissance Terrace.'

'I'd love to,' Claire replied. 'But I'm going for a swim first.' There was an awkward little silence and as Melanie glanced at Dominic Claire realised they hadn't been introduced. 'Oh,' she said, 'Melanie, this is Dominic Hansford—Dominic, Melanie Frazer.' Turning to Melanie's partner, she added, 'This is Peter Hamilton.'

As handshakes and pleasantries were exchanged Claire suddenly felt compelled to explain Dominic's presence. 'I met up with Dominic at the Trevi fountain,' she said. 'We realised we were staying here at the same hotel and he told me about tomorrow's excursion.'

Leaving her fellow guests chatting, Claire escaped and sped off to her room, taking the lift to the third floor. For some reason her spirits seemed to have lifted since she had left the hotel that morning. It must, she thought as she changed into her bikini and piled her honey-blonde hair onto the top of her head, be the experience of the Trevi or the prospect of the following day's excursion to Assisi that had done it.

She enjoyed her swim, completing several laps of the hotel's pool before returning to her room to shower and change into cropped cotton trousers and a pink top for lunch. It was as she finished drying her hair she remembered that she should have made a phone call earlier that morning but because she had left the hotel so early had postponed it.

Taking her mobile phone from her bag, she dialled a number. A male voice answered on the fourth ring. 'Mike?' she said. 'Hello, it's me.'

'Claire? Hello, darling. How's it going?'

'It's wonderful, Mike,' she replied. 'It really is. I do wish you could have come.'

'Yes, I wish I could as well.' His sigh was audible. 'But there it is. It couldn't be helped. Where have you been this morning?'

'I walked to the Spanish Steps from the hotel,' she replied, 'and then I went on to the Trevi fountain. It was magnificent, Mike—if only you could have been with me. I threw my coins in, one for luck and a second that apparently ensures my return to Rome.'

'I thought you were going to phone this morning,' he said. She caught an edge to his voice and quite suddenly could picture his expression perfectly.

'Yes, I know, I meant to,' she said quickly, 'but it was rather early when I left the hotel,' she explained.

'Emma thought you were going to phone—she was disappointed, she thought you might have wished her luck for her exam.'

'Oh, dear, I'm sorry,' Claire replied. 'Tell her I'm sorry, won't you, Mike? Is it over now? Have you heard from her?'

'No, not yet.'

'I'm going on an excursion tomorrow, Mike,' she said, deliberately changing the subject, 'to Assisi. I'm really looking forward to it. Several others from the hotel are going—Melanie and Peter, remember, the couple I told you about? And Ted and May Williams—they are a retired couple from Eastbourne who are celebrating their golden wedding anniversary and they are absolute dears…'

'Well, I hope you have a good time,' said Mike, cutting her short, 'but I'd better go now in case Emma is trying to get through.'

'Oh, yes, all right,' she said. 'Well, I'll ring again tomorrow, then. Bye, Mike.'

'Bye, Claire. I love you.'

'I love you, too,' she said, but the connection had broken and she doubted he'd even heard her.

She sat for a while staring at the phone and thinking about Mike, but it wasn't until she was on the point of leaving her room that she realised that in talking to Mike about her fellow guests she had omitted to mention Dominic Hansford. It hadn't been deliberate, she told herself. In fact, she may well have spoken of him, especially given the fact that Dominic was a doctor and that Mike would in all probability be interested in the work he did. It had simply been that Mike hadn't given her the chance, had cut her off before she'd been able to elaborate on those whom she'd befriended whilst exploring Rome. She'd tell him the next time she spoke to him, of course she would. After all, there was no reason why she shouldn't. Dominic was simply another guest, nothing more, nothing less. The fact that they were both in the medical profession had come as a pleasant surprise but it didn't mean anything.

And the fact that there had been an instant attraction between them—did that not mean anything either? she asked herself as she hurried down to lunch. Of course it didn't, she told herself firmly. Her affections lay elsewhere which hardly left her free to pursue any fanciful notions she might have had in that direction.

Nevertheless, in spite of her analysis of her acquaintance with Dominic, when she reached the hotel dining room Claire couldn't help a sudden, swift little surge of pleasure when she saw that he had been included in Melanie Frazer's lunch party.

A siesta followed the very pleasant, relaxed lunch, after which Claire, Dominic, Melanie and Peter, and Ted and May embarked on a stroll to the Piazza Navona where they sat beside the fountains, drinking Italian wine and watching the world go by.

'You will all join us for a celebration drink on our wedding anniversary, won't you?' said May after a while.

'Of course we will.' Melanie replied for them all. 'Fifty years of marriage—that's a wonderful achievement, isn't it, Peter?' she turned to her partner.

'Yes,' he nodded in agreement, 'it is, and something which I fear will become something of a rarity in years to come if the current divorce rate is anything to go by.'

'That's if couples even bother to get married in the first place,' observed Ted drily. As his wife kicked him under the table, after glancing frantically at Melanie and Peter, he looked startled then added hastily, 'Sorry, present company excepted, of course.'

'No, it's all right,' sighed Melanie. 'But I'm working on it.' She threw Peter a glance and he raised his eyes heavenwards.

'Marriage may not be such a rarity as you think,' said Dominic suddenly, and maybe because he had been mainly silent until then, everyone looked at him. 'That young couple that sit in the window in the hotel dining room,' he said, and when everyone nodded, confirming that they knew whom he meant, he went on. 'They are married—in fact, they are on their honeymoon.'

'Really?' Claire turned to him while the others all expressed surprise. 'How do you know? Did they tell you?'

Dominic shook his head. 'No,' he said, 'I saw them arrive—their room is just along the corridor from mine. He carried her over the threshold and they left a trail of confetti behind them—I think it fell out of the brim of her hat.'

'So romance isn't dead after all!' exclaimed Melanie as the others all laughed.

'Well, not in Italy it isn't,' said May.

'Mind you,' Melanie went on after a moment, 'I couldn't say the same for that other couple, Diane and Russell Hodges.' She lowered her voice and glanced over her shoulder, and the others instinctively found themselves leaning forward. 'She told me,' Melanie went on, 'that this holiday is a last-ditch attempt to save their marriage.'

Claire suddenly felt uncomfortable and sat back in her chair, not at all sure that Melanie should have divulged this information to the rest of them. It hadn't seemed to occur to Melanie that she may had been told this in confidence.

And it was there, while they were all getting to know each other a little better and under cover of the chatter from the others and the noises in the piazza, that Dominic asked Claire the inevitable question.

'Tell me,' he said casually, leaning forward in his chair so that only she could hear, 'is there a Mr Schofield?'

'No,' she replied, 'I'm not married.' She paused and looked up at him through her lashes. 'How about you?'

'Good Lord, no,' he said. 'I've never been in one place long enough to settle down.'

'I see.' Suddenly she was pleased, which was crazy because it really shouldn't make any difference to her whether Dominic was married or not.

'So,' he said softly, 'you're fancy-free?'

'I didn't say that,' she said carefully. 'You asked me if there was a Mr Schofield and I said there wasn't, but that doesn't mean there isn't anyone in my life.'

'So is there?' he asked. 'Someone in your life, I mean?'

'Yes,' she replied, 'actually, there is.' She was unable to look at him as she said it.

'Who is he?'

'His name is Mike Naylor—he's a partner in the practice where I work.'

'Not the partner who is stressed out?' Dominic raised his eyebrows.

'No, not that partner.' Claire smiled.

'More to the point,' he went on, 'what is he exactly?'

Claire frowned. 'I've just told you, he's a doctor.'

'I know,' Dominic replied. 'What I meant was, what is he to you—he isn't your husband, so is he your fiancé, your boyfriend or maybe he's your live-in lover?'

'No,' Claire shook her head, aware of the depth of interest in Dominic's dark eyes as he waited for her reply, 'we don't live together yet, and neither are we engaged...'

'So your boyfriend, then?'

'Well, yes.' She considered for a moment. 'I suppose you would call him that.'

'You don't sound too sure.' There was amusement in his eyes now and a smile played around his mouth.

He had a nice mouth, she thought, his finely shaped lips having more than a hint of sensuality about them. 'I guess I just don't think of him as that, that's all,' she said with a little shrug.

'So how do you think of him?' He was probing now, gently teasing, and she knew it.

'I don't think I want to answer that question,' she replied lightly. Then, in an effort to change the subject, she said, 'But what about you? You say you aren't married, but isn't there anyone important in your life?'

His eyes darkened slightly. 'No,' he said, 'not at the present time.'

'I find that hard to believe.' It was her turn now to tease.

'I don't see why.'

'Well, you're young and successful, you live a high-powered and exciting life. I would have thought you'd have been fighting women off.' She didn't mention the fact of his devastating good looks but in her mind that was another reason for surprise at his single status.

'I should be so lucky.' He shrugged. 'It doesn't work that way. Women don't seem to like the fact that I'm not in the same place for any length of time.'

Claire had no chance to comment further for Melanie suddenly leaned forward. 'What do *you* do, Dominic?' she said, breaking into their conversation, and Claire realised the topic had changed from marriage to jobs.

His hesitation before answering may have been imperceptible to anyone else but Claire noticed it. 'I work for various charities,' he replied, 'helping to set up their organisations overseas, that sort of thing.'

His answer seemed to satisfy Melanie, but later, as they strolled back through the side streets for dinner at their hotel and Claire found Dominic at her side, she said softly, 'Why didn't you tell them what you really do?'

'Because if I do I will find that someone invariably wants a second opinion on some long-standing condition,' he replied simply.

'But you told me when I asked,' Claire replied.

'Ah,' he said, 'I know. But you were different, and I knew that.'

For some obscure reason his reply gave her a warm glow inside.

CHAPTER TWO

'MAY I join you?'

'Of course.'

Barely waiting for Claire's answer, Dominic lowered himself into the seat alongside her. It was the following morning and after a very early breakfast the group from the hotel had made their way into the piazza where they were picked up by a coach which was already half-full with guests from other hotels in the vicinity who were all making the trip to Assisi. Melanie and Peter were settling themselves across the gangway while Ted and May were in the seats immediately behind.

'Aye, aye,' muttered Peter, just loud enough for those around him to hear, 'here come the honeymooners—didn't think they would be gracing us with their company at this ungodly hour.' They all watched, smiling as the young couple, whose names Claire had learnt in the bar the night before were Rob and Nicola Moore, climbed the steps of the coach and collapsed into the nearest seats as if the exertion was all too much for them. They were followed by Diane and Russell Hodges, who pushed their way to the rear of the coach to sit with those from other hotels rather than ones from their own party. Diane, dressed in jeans and a bright orange top, was tight-lipped while beneath the brim of his sunhat Russell wore his usual morose expression.

'Looks like those two have wasted their money,' observed Peter.

'Shh!' said Melanie. 'They'll hear you.'

'They can't hear me,' said Peter. 'I thought you said this

trip was intended to put their marriage right,' he added after a moment.

'That's what she told me,' said Melanie.

'Well, it isn't working, is it?' Peter leaned across the aisle towards Dominic. 'Whatever it is he's done, she's not going to give an inch.'

'Give them time,' said Dominic. 'Let Italy work its magic.'

The guide that day was a young Italian woman who introduced herself as Luisa and told them that their driver, with his black curls and laughing dark eyes, was Guiseppe. He turned and greeted them merrily in Italian, and as his passengers murmured a reply Claire noticed that hanging from the driving mirror was a crucifix on a chain and a rosary of black beads.

Rome was only just coming to life as they left the piazza. On one corner a flower seller was filling the shelves of her stall with masses of blooms—vivid swathes of colour against the sienna tones of the buildings—while at the café on the opposite corner the proprietor was setting out his tables and chairs beneath a striped awning. Through the open window of the coach Claire caught the unmistakable aroma of rich dark coffee, and as they turned into the main road they passed two black-garbed priests hurrying through the almost deserted streets.

'I don't think I know another city where ancient and modern seem to merge so subtly,' said Dominic as they sped through the streets of Rome. 'On the one hand are the remains of that once glorious civilisation and on the other the buildings and shops of the modern world with their designer labels and expensive goods.'

They left the city to a cacophony of bells from the many churches and cathedrals calling the faithful to early morning mass, and as they headed for the hills that surround

Rome the sun was penetrating the early mist like a huge lemon orb in a sky of pale turquoise.

'We didn't have your storm,' observed Claire as they settled down in their seats for the journey ahead.

'No,' Dominic agreed. 'Not yet.'

'You still think we might?'

'Maybe. Possibly.' He shrugged.

'But it's a lovely morning,' she protested. 'It's so still—look, there's not a breath of wind.'

'I know,' he agreed then added, 'It's going to be hot.'

'I've brought my sunhat,' said Claire, 'and sun cream. I don't want to burn—I started to yesterday.'

'You've covered up a bit today—very sensible.' He glanced at her ankle-length cotton skirt and white top then at her long hair, which she had tied back with a lilac-coloured chiffon scarf.

'It wasn't only being sensible,' said Claire, feeling her cheeks grow warm under his scrutiny. 'I've found that some buildings, particularly the churches, won't allow entry if you're wearing shorts or if women have bare shoulders.'

'So I believe.' Dominic nodded and she stole a sideways glance at him. Today he was wearing a pair of cream chinos and a red shirt, a striking a contrast to his dark eyes and hair.

They fell silent for a time, the city behind them now as they travelled through acres of olive groves and vineyards and into the vast rolling expanse of the Umbrian countryside. After a while Luisa brought coffee or fruit juice and tiny almond-flavoured biscuits, and as they sipped and nibbled she pointed out landmarks and explained local history and points of interest. She went on to tell them that they would be visiting a hilltop village where they would stop for light refreshment before travelling on to a monastery and museum high in the hills before reaching their final destination of Assisi, the birthplace of Saint Francis, where they would have lunch and spend a few hours.

'Tell me about your doctor,' said Dominic suddenly, as Luisa switched off her microphone and the sound of her voice was replaced by a softly played recording of a Puccini aria.

'What do you want to know?' Claire threw him a startled glance.

'Well, for a start, what is he thinking of, letting you come here alone?'

'I'm quite capable of travelling alone,' she protested indignantly.

'I don't doubt that,' he replied swiftly. 'In fact, I'm sure you are. But I have to say if I was him I wouldn't have been too happy at letting you loose among all these Italian Romeos—to say nothing of predatory English tourists,' he added drily.

'Do you include yourself in that?' she asked lightly.

He grinned. 'Maybe.'

'So could I be at risk in your company?' She threw him an amused glance.

'You could well be. A lovely young woman like you...' He trailed off, the sentence unfinished. 'But, seriously, why isn't he with you?' His smile disappeared, to be replaced by a puzzled frown. 'First time Rome is an experience to be shared—especially by lovers.'

'I'm sure you are right.' She sighed. 'And that was the way it was supposed to have been. Mike was originally coming with me but at the last minute something happened and he had to pull out. Rather than cancel my ticket as well, I decided to come alone.'

'Must have been something pretty drastic to make him cancel,' Dominic observed.

'Well, yes, I suppose it was really.' Claire wrinkled her nose. 'It was his daughter...' she said after a moment.

'His daughter?' There was an edge of surprise in Dominic's voice now.

'Yes—Mike's divorced. He has an eleven-year-old daughter and a thirteen-year-old son who live with their mother,' she explained. 'They visit Mike quite often... Anyway, just before we were due to leave, Mike's ex-wife was called away suddenly and Emma and Stephen had to come to stay with their father. At first we wondered if they could have come to Rome with us but their mother said it was out of the question because Emma had a couple of important exams this week.'

'So was there no one else they could have stayed with?' There was the slightest note of incredulity in Dominic's voice now and Claire found herself defending the decision.

'No, not really.' She shook her head, recalling Emma's tears and her mother's indignation when that had been suggested.

'Well, I think if I'd been their father I would have found some alternative,' said Dominic.

'It's not that easy,' said Claire, shaking her head. 'You don't understand. Mike has his obligations to his family...'

'I'm sure he does. I guess he also has obligations to you if he's having a relationship with you.'

'Well, yes,' Claire agreed, 'but I knew the score when I started seeing Mike. I knew he had children.' She had grown used to playing second fiddle to Stephen and Emma and it surprised her now to find someone who obviously didn't think she always should.

'So was he already divorced?' Dominic threw her a glance when she didn't immediately answer. 'Sorry,' he added, 'you don't have to answer that. Just tell me to mind my own business if you like.'

'No, it's OK,' said Claire, surprised to find that she really didn't mind. Usually she didn't like discussing her private life with anyone and certainly not details of Mike's domestic arrangements, but somehow, sitting here beside Dominic as they sped away from Rome on this glorious summer's day, home seemed very far away and it seemed the most natural thing in the world. 'Yes,' she said, 'Mike was already divorced when I came to work at the Hargreaves Centre—I'm not a home-wrecker, you know.'

'I didn't for one moment imagine you were,' he said drily.

'His wife, Jan, had left him,' she went on, 'and taken the children and gone to live with a colleague—she's a teacher,' she added. 'Mike was apparently devastated at the time, or so I've heard, but eventually he agreed to a divorce. I came along afterwards and we gradually started seeing one another.'

'And the ex-wife, did she marry her teacher?' Dominic raised one eyebrow.

'No.' Claire shook her head. 'He left her shortly after the divorce.'

'And how did Mike take that?'

'Well, by then he was saying he wouldn't take Jan back if she was the last woman on earth.'

'And what about you and he?' asked Dominic softly. 'Do you have long-term plans in all this?'

'Yes,' Claire replied slowly, 'Mike and I are thinking of moving in together soon. But I don't think he would be in a hurry to rush into marriage for a second time...'

'So where does that leave you?' he asked.

'I'm happy with the situation,' she replied lightly, 'and it suits me the way it is, at least for the time being.'

'It doesn't exactly sound like an affair that's going to set the world alight,' observed Dominic.

'Maybe not...' Claire shrugged. 'But it's safe and easy-going and—'

'And it suits you?' He finished the sentence for her and she suspected he was mocking her slightly.

'Yes, it suits me,' she said firmly. She leaned forward. 'Look,' she said, 'Peter's offering us sweets.' She was glad of the interruption, glad that something was steering them off the conversation, which had suddenly made her feel uneasy. She had been completely comfortable with it right up until Dominic had somehow implied that she couldn't possibly be satisfied with what must have sounded to him like a very lukewarm relationship. Taking a sweet from the bag that was being offered, she unwrapped it and popped it into her mouth then turned away from Dominic and stared out of the window.

So was it merely lukewarm, her relationship with Mike? She was happy when she was with him, she knew that. She also knew she would never want to hurt him, especially in view of how much he had already been through, but did she love him? Of course she did, she told herself firmly as she began sucking her sweet. If she didn't she would hardly be having a relationship with him. Dominic knew nothing about it, nothing about Mike or about her, so he was scarcely in a position to judge.

'Actually...' Dominic unwrapped his own sweet, having, at an indication from Peter, passed the bag back to Ted and May '...I'm rather grateful to whoever called Mike's ex-wife away at the last moment.'

'Oh?' Claire half turned her head to look at him and at the expression in his eyes, to her dismay, felt her cheeks growing warm.

'Yes,' he said calmly, 'because if he had come I would hardly be sitting here beside you, enjoying your company. I would have been back there beside Archie as that is the only empty seat.' Archie was a student who was studying the history of art and who was also travelling alone.

'And what's wrong with Archie?' murmured Claire, glancing over her shoulder at the bespectacled, rather intense-looking young man who was earnestly studying a map.

'Nothing,' said Dominic, 'absolutely nothing. From what I've seen of him he's a very nice chap but, given the choice, I'd far rather be sitting here with you.'

At that moment, to Claire's relief, Luisa switched on her microphone again and she attempted to concentrate on what the guide was saying about the history of a walled town they were passing high on the horizon, the outline of its towers and buildings sharply etched against the blue sky.

After a while she dozed then when she came to it was to find that they were passing through rich acres of farmland dotted with solid, square, slate-roofed farmhouses and bordered by long columns of tall, thin, dark green, cypress trees.

'Typically Italian,' murmured Dominic at her side.

An hour later Claire realised that they had been climbing steadily for some considerable time and the landscape had changed yet again, this time to densely wooded hillsides and deep ravines as they left the gentle farmlands far below.

'There's the village we're going to.' Dominic leaned forward suddenly and pointed to a cluster of ancient umber and sienna buildings that seemed to be clinging precariously to the hillside. Even as he spoke the coach took a sharp left-hand bend, Guiseppe changed to the lowest possible gear and it began climbing the last few kilometres to the hilltop village.

The coach came to a halt in a small car park and everyone stumbled out, stretching limbs and flexing muscles and only half listening to Luisa who told them that they had an hour to visit one of the village's tiny cafés, explore the ancient church and buildings and admire the view.

'It's hot,' said Claire, clamping her straw sunhat onto her head as together with Melanie and Peter, she and Dominic climbed a short, very steep, rocky path to a stone parapet that provided a viewing platform.

'Just look at that view,' said Peter.

The four of them stood in awe and gazed out across the landscape, which stretched for as far as the eye could see to some unknown far distant horizon. From below somewhere a single bell tolled, its melancholy notes echoing across the countryside. Once again Claire was aware of a stillness in the air, that same stillness that Dominic had felt could be the forerunner of a storm and which this time was coupled with a clarity of vision that enabled them to see even the distant hills and far-flung villages in heightened detail, where one might have expected a shimmering haze, given the heat of the day.

And suddenly, in spite of the heat and the startling blueness of the sky, Claire shivered. Turning away from the view, she made her way back down the path to find May at the bottom. 'Be careful if you're going up,' she told the older woman. 'It's very uneven underfoot.'

'I think I might pass on this one,' said May. 'Are you going to look at the church?'

'Yes, I thought I would,' Claire replied.

'In that case, I'll come with you,' said May. 'Ted's gone to find the gents,' she explained.

Together with May, Claire made her way through the village to the tiny whitewashed church with its single bell tower.

'Luisa said there's a fine altar in here with a wonderful painting of the Last Supper,' said May. 'I particularly wanted to see it.'

As they entered the cool dimness of the church they found Archie was there before them and within minutes Dominic, Melanie and Peter caught them up and they spent the next ten minutes or so admiring the simple beauty of the tiny place of worship—the painting, which indeed was impressive, the statues, the fresh lilies and the crisp, white, lace-edged altar linen.

It was a moment of calm and peace, coolness away from the searing heat of the day, and long afterwards Claire was to remember it, but for the moment it held no more significance other than the tranquillity of a devotedly cared-for place of worship.

In no time at all it seemed they were back in the coach and on the road once more, this time covering the few kilometres to the hilltop monastery that was to be their final port of call before Assisi.

It briefly occurred to Claire as Dominic took his place beside her that the others seemed to be treating them as a couple. Maybe she should be saying something to dissuade that, she thought, and then she dismissed the idea. After all, what did it matter? She knew it wasn't so, and so did Dominic—he more than knew by now her involvement with Mike, so really it didn't matter what anyone else might think. Besides, after this holiday she would probably never see any of these people again.

If, as she at first thought, this realisation was meant to be some sort of reassurance, she couldn't immediately understand why she felt suddenly depressed by the prospect as once again she clambered from the coach. But then, and even without scrutinising the matter too closely, she knew that it wasn't the prospect of not seeing any of the others again, pleasant as they were, that depressed her, it was more the thought that she might never see Dominic again.

The monastery, built in the Middle Ages, was no longer in use as a retreat. Time and weather had played their part in its deterioration and the community had long since moved to more appropriate accommodation in nearby Assisi, but it wasn't difficult to imagine how it once might have been.

Luisa had told them before they had left the coach that

much of the monastery, including the monks' cells and living quarters, was unsafe and no longer open to the public, but the church and the cloisters were still open, together with the large refectory which these days served as a museum of local art and artefacts. She'd gone on to say that they had half an hour before they would move on to Assisi.

'I think I would have liked longer here,' said Claire as they made their way up the hill on foot to the buildings at the top.

'Whatever for?' demanded Melanie, puffing slightly from the steepness of the road. 'There's nothing much here, only some dusty old museum.'

'And a church,' said May, pausing for breath.

'Well, that goes without saying,' said Melanie drily. 'Everywhere we go there's a church.'

'I know,' said Claire, also pausing and looking up at the buildings of yellowish stone that soared above them and the mass of pink and white flowers that bordered the road and even grew in the crevices between the stones. 'I just thought it was rather nice here, that's all.'

'That's probably what the monks thought all those years ago when they decided to make their home here,' observed Dominic.

They all paused for a moment, really to give Ted and May the chance to catch up, and as Claire looked back down the road she saw that several members of the party had decided to join them, including Diane and Russell, and other guests Rob and Nicola, but that others had elected to stay near the coach, some sitting on the grass in the shade of a cluster of fig trees with Luisa and Guiseppe.

'Are you both all right?' Dominic asked as Ted and May reached them.

'Yes, fine.' May nodded. Her face was bright red from the heat and the exertion but she was still smiling. 'I'm determined to get there—I really want to see this. But one good thing—if I collapse, at least we have a nurse with us.' She looked at Claire as she spoke.

'You told them,' murmured Dominic a little later as they approached the outer gates of the monastery.

'I didn't have a lot of choice,' Claire replied. 'They asked me what I did for a living and I couldn't lie to them, neither am I able to cloak it in ambiguity as you do.'

Dominic laughed, then, as she would have stumbled on the uneven ground, he took her arm to steady her. At the touch of his fingers on her bare arm she jumped. She could only liken the experience to that of an electric shock she had once received from a faulty iron. It must be the strange atmosphere again, she thought, that stillness they had remarked on before—either that or the altitude they were at, high in the Apennines, that caused that electric feeling.

They passed through the monastery gates, across a large courtyard and into the stillness of the church. It was dim inside and almost cold after the intense heat of the sun. They found themselves talking in whispers, which seemed to echo around the ancient stone walls. Statues stood shrouded in shadows and it was almost a relief to move through a doorway to the left of the sanctuary, out of the gloom and into the cloisters whose high, arched stone columns looked out over a garden bathed in sunlight obviously still well tended with its pencil-thin conifers, orange trees and boxed hedges. Windows in the buildings that towered around the garden were either bricked in or boarded up, giving the place a rather sad, desolate air. Two elderly custodians who were on duty directed the party round two sides of the cloisters and into a large building at the end.

'This must have been the refectory,' said Dominic, as he and Claire paused for a moment and stood looking up at the rafters in the vaulted roof space of the huge room. 'You can imagine the monks sitting here in rows each day, silently eating their food.'

'I can't imagine anyone wanting to shut themselves away from the world like that,' said Melanie with a shudder.

'Oh, I don't know,' muttered Russell, who had entered the building behind them. 'It has its attractions.'

Around the walls of the vast room on trestle tables were numerous exhibits from local sculptors, artists and stonemasons, and it was as Claire and Dominic and the rest of their group had moved to the far end of the room and were gazing in awe at a dais of at least a dozen life-size stone figures of saints that they heard the first rumbling sounds.

At first Claire thought it was thunder and she turned to Dominic. 'Looks like you were right,' she said, 'about there being a storm on the way, although I have to say I can hardly believe it—why, there wasn't so much as a cloud in the sky when we came in…' She trailed off as she caught sight of Dominic's expression.

'What is it?' she said, uneasy now by the look of anxious alarm on his face.

'That isn't thunder,' he muttered.

'Then what is it?'

By this time others had heard it and were turning from the exhibits and exclaiming to each other.

'I think we should get outside,' said Dominic. 'Everyone get to the door,' he called, raising his voice so that the others all looked towards him while the ominous rumbling sound grew louder by the second.

'What is it?' gasped Melanie, clutching at Peter's arm.

'It sounds like an earth tremor,' said Dominic. 'I experienced one once when I was in Brazil.' By this time everyone was moving in a mass across the vast room towards the door.

'But it can't be,' cried Diane. 'They don't have earthquakes in Italy.'

'Oh, yes, they do,' said Archie. 'They've had them in this region recently as well…' Even as he spoke the building began to shake and the ground started to move and tilt. There were screams from a couple of the women and Dominic instinctively put his arm around Claire, holding her close as, transfixed, they waited for the moment to pass.

When the noise and shaking subsided Dominic spoke again, his voice carrying authority as he assumed leadership. 'Come on,' he urged, 'let's get outside.'

They had only just begun to move when there came another earth-shattering roar, much louder this time, and as the building shook and shuddered for a second time, wooden rafters and great chunks of masonry came crashing down in front of them.

Claire screamed in terror. Dominic pulled her into his arms and, throwing her to the floor, shielded her with his body as hell itself seemed to erupt around them and stone, wood and plaster crashed to the ground.

CHAPTER THREE

IT SEEMED to go on for hours when in actual fact it couldn't have been more than a few minutes. All that Claire was aware of was the weight of Dominic's body over hers, the darkness as he covered her face with his arm and the overwhelming sense of terror as she became convinced she was about to die.

Then, as if someone had thrown a switch, thoughts began to teem through her brain. She thought of her father and of how it would be for him when he was told that she had died in an earthquake. She thought of Mike and wondered if he would at last think that he should have gone with her. Would he feel guilty? Would it be a guilt that he would carry with him to his grave or would he simply be thankful that he hadn't been with her? And Emma and Stephen—he would most certainly be thankful that they hadn't gone. They would now just get on with the rest of their lives without her and maybe, in time, they might even forget her…

'Are you all right?' Dominic's voice was muffled as if he were speaking through a thick blanket. 'Claire…?' He moved then and Claire realised that the dreadful rumbling noises had stopped, replaced by silence, an eerie, deafening silence. So she wasn't dead after all. If she was, then Dominic had died as well and they were still together. The thought, obscure as it was, somehow was infinitely comforting.

'I think…so.' She moved her head, aware now of the clouds of choking dust around them.

Cautiously Dominic eased himself away from her and

Claire could see that he was covered in the thick white dust. The enveloping silence was as profound as ever but as Claire lay for a moment on her back and gazed up, the dust cleared a little and she could see that a huge section of the roof had fallen in and the intense blue of the Italian sky was visible. Even as she lay there, she heard a brief snatch of birdsong. Turning her head, she saw that Dominic was crawling across the floor towards what looked like a bundle of rags covered in thick dust and it was then she heard other sounds—the sound of groaning, human voices muttering in bewilderment or frantic with urgency, a woman's sudden hysterical sobbing.

Somehow Claire managed to struggle to her knees and as she looked around her she saw that the choking dust was beginning to settle. Two huge stone pillars had collapsed and an enormous section of the ceiling and roof had crashed into the old refectory, forming a huge mound of rubble between where Claire and Dominic had huddled for safety and the main entrance. Other figures were stirring now, everyone covered in several layers of the white dust. Claire saw Archie stumbling across the floor in front of her and suddenly Melanie was beside her, coughing and choking.

'Claire…' she gasped, 'where's Peter? I can't find him. Oh, God, where is he? Peter!' her voice rose to a wail.

Claire turned and looked to where Dominic was crouched over the bundle on the ground. Was that Peter? Even as she thought the unthinkable, wondering how she would cope with Melanie if it proved to be so, Dominic crawled back. 'There's nothing I can do for him,' he said.

'Oh, my God!' Melanie's hands flew to her mouth. 'Peter!' She would have crawled through the rubble but Dominic restrained her.

'It isn't Peter,' he said.

'Who is it?' Claire looked over his shoulder and saw that

a rafter had fallen across the body and was partly obscuring its head and neck.

'I don't know,' Dominic replied. 'It must be someone from one of the other hotels or perhaps someone who works here. Whoever it is, he took the full force of that rafter on his head—he must have died instantly.'

'But where is Peter?' wailed Melanie.

'Mel?' Suddenly, like an apparition, Peter was there beside them. There was a gash on his forehead and through the white, chalky dust his face was streaked with blood.

'Oh, Peter!' Melanie collapsed into his arms. 'I thought you were dead.'

'No,' he replied shakily, 'of course I'm not dead. It would take more than some earthquake to kill me off.'

'That man is dead.' Melanie glanced fearfully over her shoulder.

'Is he?' Peter sounded shocked, his air of bravado abandoned now in the face of grim reality. 'Are we sure? I mean, are we certain there isn't anything we can do for him?'

'Well, Dominic said he was...' Melanie glanced at Dominic.

'Even so...I think perhaps...' Peter began, but Dominic cut him short.

'He's dead,' he said quietly. 'Believe me, there's nothing anyone can do. I'm a doctor,' he added when it seemed that Peter might be about to argue the point further.

Peter threw him a quick, surprised glance. 'Do we know who it is?' he asked after a moment.

'No.' It was Melanie who replied. 'We think he may be from one of the other hotels... But where are the others?' Wildly she glanced around. 'We weren't the only ones in here when it happened...'

'I saw Archie just now,' said Claire. 'He seemed OK...'

'Ted and May—where are they?' Melanie looked round, peering through the dust-choked atmosphere.

'I'll go and see if I can find them,' said Dominic.

'I'll come with you,' said Peter.

'No,' Dominic replied swiftly. 'You stay here with the girls.' Stepping towards Peter, he peered at the gash on his forehead, which was seeping blood now at an alarming rate. 'Claire…' he half turned to her '…see if you can do anything to stop this bleeding.'

'Yes, of course.' Claire pulled her bag towards her, which luckily had been underneath her when Dominic had pulled them to the ground so had escaped much of the dust, and began rummaging inside as Dominic began clambering over the fallen rafters and huge chunks of masonry.

Inside her bag she found a new packet of wet wipes, which she tore open. Peter lowered himself to the floor and she knelt beside him and, using one of the wipes, gently cleansed the area around the wound. Taking a wad of clean tissues from her bag, she pressed it to the wound, applying pressure in an attempt to staunch the flow of blood. 'It needs stitches really,' she said, 'but we'll have to make do with the next best thing.'

Suddenly Dominic was back beside them. 'Claire,' he said, 'I need you to give me a hand. Melanie,' he went on urgently, 'take the pad from Claire and keep it pressed to the wound.'

'What's happening?' asked Peter, peering up at Dominic from beneath the pad of tissues.

'Well, the entrance is completely blocked,' Dominic replied. 'A couple of the guys are trying to see if there's another way out.'

'What about Ted and May?' asked Melanie.

'Ted is injured,' Dominic replied briefly, 'and May has cuts and bruises. There are others who are injured as well but I haven't got to them yet.'

Scrambling to her feet, Claire took Dominic's outstretched hand and carefully began picking her way through the debris to a far corner of the refectory. Behind great chunks of plaster and stone she found Ted lying half-propped against the wall with May beside him. The older man's teeth were clenched in pain, his eyes were closed and his face, beneath his thatch of thick white hair, appeared ashen even through the dust, which clogged his mouth and nostrils and spiked his eyelashes.

'The falling stonework crushed his thigh,' murmured Dominic to Claire. 'I managed to lift it but I think he has a fractured femur. I want you to help me to straighten it and if we can, we'll try and find something to immobilise it.' He glanced up and saw that Archie was crouching beside May. He, too, was covered in dust and his glasses were cracked. 'Archie,' Dominic went on, 'maybe you could do that. Find something for a couple of splints if you can.'

'Right.' Archie scrambled to his feet and disappeared behind the huge mound of rubble.

'Ted, we're going to try to make you a bit more comfortable,' Dominic began, breaking off as Russell suddenly appeared at their side, his expression wild. 'Russell?' he said. 'What is it?'

'Where's Diane?' Russell stared at Claire and irrelevantly she noticed he had lost his straw hat.

'I don't know.' Claire shook her head.

'I thought she was with you.' The wild expression in Russell's eyes turned to one of panic. 'The last I saw of her she was looking at those statues and you were beside her—I'm sure you were...'

'No...' Claire shook her head and at that moment a sudden shout went up.

'Can we have some help? Over here, please. Anybody. There's someone trapped under this lot.'

'Oh, my God! Diane!' Russell turned and began clambering back over the rubble.

'We should help,' said Dominic. 'Lie still, Ted. We'll be back, May. Stay with him.'

'I'm not going anywhere,' said May, calmly kneeling beside her husband and gently stroking his hand.

Someone was indeed buried under a heap of fallen rubble and a group of at least eight people, including Archie, Dominic, Claire, Russell and Rob Moore, began tearing at the chunks of masonry and wood with their bare hands. As they worked frantically, Claire caught a glimpse of orange-coloured material and even before they finally pulled the person free from the rubble she knew that it was indeed Diane.

By the time they had eased her clear of the rubble and laid her on the floor and Dominic was able to examine her, Russell was almost beside himself with anxiety.

'Oh, God,' he cried as he stood helplessly, wringing his hands, 'is she all right? She's not dead, is she? Oh, please, say she isn't dead.'

From the appearance of Diane's limp body, closed eyes, white face and blood-soaked hair, it looked as if she could well be dead and momentarily Claire's heart went out to Russell in his moment of anguish. Then her professionalism took over as she and Dominic worked over Diane to clear her airways and search for a pulse.

'She's alive,' said Dominic at last, 'but she's had a severe blow to her head and she's unconscious.'

'Oh, thank heavens.' Russell crouched down beside the inert figure of his wife. 'But is she going to be all right?' he demanded.

'I hope so,' Dominic replied. 'But it rather depends on how soon we can get her out of this place and into a hospital. Claire, can you do anything with this wound?'

Claire had slipped the packet of wipes into the pocket of

her skirt before leaving Peter and she retrieved them now. Taking a couple from the packet, she knelt on the ground and began to cleanse the wound, which looked larger and deeper than that suffered by Peter and which was oozing blood at an alarming rate. 'Has anyone got anything I can use as a pad?' she asked. 'Clean tissues or handkerchiefs?'

'Will this do?' Nicola produced a white cotton T-shirt from her bag. 'I always carry a spare.'

'That's brilliant,' said Claire, taking the garment from her, folding it and pressing it to the side of Diane's head.

'Has anyone found another way out of this place?' asked Dominic, looking round.

'No.' It was a large, burly-looking man with a very red face who Claire vaguely remembered seeing on the coach who answered. 'The entrance, as you know, is completely blocked. There is another door at the far end of the room. We managed to reach it but we could only open it a few inches because there appears to be something behind it. At a guess I would say it's more rubble.'

'So what can we do?' asked Nicola Moore fearfully.

'Does anyone have a mobile phone?' asked Dominic.

There were sudden mutterings and scrabblings amongst the others as if until that moment it actually hadn't occurred to anyone to use their mobiles. Several people produced phones while there were cries of dismay from others who found they had left theirs aboard the coach. Two mobiles, including Claire's, had been damaged, another couldn't receive any signal and the only one that appeared to be working belonged to Rob.

'Who shall I try?' he asked in sudden bewilderment as everyone waited for him to dial.

'What about the hotel?' said someone. 'I've got the number here on one of their cards.'

'There's no reply,' said Rob after dialling the number

and waiting while everyone watched in an agony of suspense.

'What about the emergency number?' said someone.

'OK.' Rob dialled 999. 'I hope it's the same as ours,' he said, then a moment later added, 'Well, even if it is, I can't get through. Trouble is, even if I did, I doubt my Italian would be good enough to be able to tell anyone where we are.' He paused and looked round at the others for inspiration.

'You could always try phoning England,' said Claire suddenly. 'I read about someone who was shipwrecked off China who rang his family in England. They contacted their local coastguard who mounted a rescue operation and he was saved.'

'Good idea,' said Rob. 'I'll try it.'

'Who are you phoning?' asked Nicola, leaning over his shoulder.

'My dad,' he replied.

Moments later Rob had told his father about their predicament and their location and his father said he would phone the police with the details.

'What do we do now?' asked Melanie after Rob had rung off.

'Nothing.' It was Dominic who replied. 'We sit tight until the emergency services get through to us—which they will, in time. Those outside—Luisa and Guiseppe and the others on the coach—know we are in here. They will have sent for help and if they haven't then, thanks to Rob, the English police will have got on to the Italian authorities.'

'But it was an earthquake, wasn't it?' said Nicola, and there was a trace of hysteria in her voice now. 'What if it's affected everyone—what if the others are dead or injured, what if there aren't any emergency services left to get through?' Her voice rose and Rob put his arm around her in an attempt to comfort his young wife.

'That's highly unlikely,' Dominic replied calmly. All the while they had been talking he had been examining Diane's limbs for any further injuries. 'Especially in this area,' he went on. 'It is more likely to be severe earth tremors which have caused some structural damage instead of a full-scale earthquake.'

His words seemed to have a calming effect on Nicola but it was obvious that everyone was well aware that there was a possibility, however remote, that they just might be trapped in this place for some considerable length of time.

'I think there is some damage to her shoulder,' Dominic said at last, looking at Russell and rising to his feet. 'I can't be certain, of course, without an X-ray.'

Taking another of the wipes, which had suddenly become extremely precious, Claire began cleaning the dust from Diane's mouth and nose. She had almost finished when she heard a voice behind her.

'Will these do?' Claire glanced over her shoulder and found Archie standing there with two pieces of wood in his hands. 'They're a couple of the legs from one of the trestle tables.'

'Excellent,' said Dominic. 'If you've finished there, Claire, we'll try and get these splints onto Ted's leg.'

Leaving Diane with Russell and Nicola, who continued to apply pressure on Diane's head wound, Dominic and Claire returned to Ted. Between them they managed to immobilise his leg with the two pieces of wood, binding them together with strips of fabric torn from Rob's and Archie's shirts. By the time they had finished Ted was in terrible pain and Dominic asked if anyone had any form of pain relief with them.

'I've got some paracetamol tablets,' said May, 'but I don't think Ted with be able to get them down without water.'

'I've got a can of Coke,' said Rob, producing his rucksack.

'That'll do,' Dominic replied, taking the bottle of pain-killers from May and shaking a couple into the palm of his hand while Rob pulled the ring on the soft-drink can. Between them Dominic and Claire managed to persuade Ted to take the tablets and wash them down with a few mouthfuls of Coke. 'I suggest,' said Dominic as he returned the can to Rob, 'that you save that. We may well be glad of it later.'

'You're obviously a doctor.' The big man with the red face was back, and when Dominic nodded he said, 'I think you'd better take a look at a lady over there. She and her sister are staying at the same hotel as me and she seems to be in a lot of discomfort.'

Dominic stood up. 'Where is she?' he said.

'At the back of the room,' said the man. 'I don't think either of them have been injured but, like I say, one of them seems to be in some sort of trouble.'

'I'll come with you,' said Claire. Looking at the couple on the ground, she said, 'May, you care for Ted. I'll be back soon.'

Following the man, Claire and Dominic made their way to the very back of the large room. As they did so the full extent of the damage became evident, from the huge portion of the roof that had collapsed and caved in to a section of the outer wall that was bulging precariously and looked as if it might be about to topple. Claire shuddered as she realised for the first time how fortunate they were to be alive and how easily the whole building could have collapsed and buried them all beneath the rubble.

The two elderly sisters were huddled in the shelter of an upturned trestle table and one of them looked up, her expression one of hope at the man who had brought Dominic and Claire and whom she obviously knew.

'Dorothy.' The man leaned forward, resting his hands on his knees and puffing slightly from exertion and the choking dust that still permeated the air. 'This man is a doctor. I've asked him to take a look at Evelyn for you.'

'Thank you, Desmond,' the lady replied. 'I am rather concerned about her.' They spoke as if this were any mid-afternoon surgery in an English provincial town instead of the life-and-death situation in which they all found themselves in the aftermath of an earthquake, high in the Italian hills and miles away from the nearest town.

Dominic nodded and smiled at the lady then crouched down beside her sister. 'Hello, Evelyn,' he said. 'I'm Dominic Hansford and I'm a doctor.'

Claire, looking down at the lady called Evelyn, noticed that she was having trouble with her breathing and that her fingers were clutching at the front of her blouse as if she was in pain.

'She suffers from a heart condition,' explained Dorothy. 'She took her medication this morning but she seems to be in a lot of distress at the moment.'

'Does she have anything with her?' asked Dominic as he took Evelyn's pulse. 'Any tablets, or a spray for angina?'

Dorothy nodded. 'Yes, she has both but unfortunately they are in her bag in the coach…'

Claire knew that without medication for the pain and oxygen to assist with her breathing, all they could do was to try to make Evelyn as comfortable as possible until her angina attack passed. Once again at a signal from Dominic she took the wet wipes from her pocket and proceeded to clean Evelyn's face and moisten her dry lips.

'She's rather clammy,' Claire murmured to Dominic as she finished.

'We need to keep her warm,' he replied. 'The trouble is, it was so hot outside no one was wearing much in the way of warm clothing.'

What he said was true. Most of the women, including the two sisters, were wearing thin dresses or skirts and tops while the men were in shorts or cotton trousers and shirts.

'I'm so thirsty...' whispered Evelyn.

Dominic stood up. 'I'm going to get everyone to pool resources,' he said. 'Failing anyone producing anything better, I'll bring back Rob's can of Coke.'

He disappeared back in to the main body of the refectory, leaving Claire to comfort Evelyn and to keep her as calm as possible, encouraging her to ride her pain instead of fighting it.

'Do you think someone will come to rescue us?' whispered Dorothy after a while.

'I don't know,' Claire replied truthfully. 'We can only hope so.'

'I blame myself for this,' Dorothy went on, gazing helplessly at her sister and gently chafing one of her hands between her own. 'I was looking after her bag for her and I put it in the compartment above our seats, thinking it was too heavy for her to carry around. I never thought about her medication—I should have done, I know how much she depends on it—but all I could think about was that I wanted to see this monastery because a friend at home had told me to be sure not to miss it. I feel terrible now.'

'You mustn't blame yourself, Dorothy,' said Claire gently. 'There was no way you could have known what was going to happen—there was no way any of us could have known.'

'They had earthquakes in this area a few years ago, you know,' said Dorothy. 'Assisi was badly hit, especially the basilica.'

'So I believe,' said Claire. 'I remember seeing that on the news now but I still say there wasn't any way we could have known about this.'

'No, maybe not.' Dorothy shook her head and Claire saw

a tear trickle down her cheek, making a rivulet in the dust. 'Are you a doctor as well?' she asked Claire after a moment.

'No,' Claire shook her head, 'I'm a nurse, though.'

'How fortunate we are to have you with us, and that nice young doctor.'

As if on cue, Dominic was suddenly back, a small plastic bottle in one hand and some sort of garment in the other. 'I've done a little better than soft drink this time,' he said to Claire. 'Someone had this bottle of mineral water and May had this cardigan in her bag.' He stooped down beside Evelyn and covered her with the white cardigan then, unscrewing the cap, he held the bottle to her lips while gently supporting her neck with his other hand as she managed to take a few sips.

As she watched him Claire suddenly realised that there was a dark patch on the back of his shirt around one shoulder blade. Reaching out her hand, she touched it and found it was wet and that the shirt was torn.

At the touch of her hand he glanced up at her over his shoulder. 'What is it?' he said.

'You're bleeding, Dominic,' she said. 'I didn't notice it before on your red shirt.'

'It's nothing,' he said dismissively, getting to his feet and replacing the cap on the bottle. 'Just a graze, that's all.'

'I think you'd better let me be the judge of that,' Claire replied firmly. 'Come on—over here, and let me take a look.'

Surprisingly he didn't argue any further, following Claire away from Dorothy and Evelyn and into the light from a tall window, its glass shattered in the tremor. She watched as he undid the buttons on his shirt and as he made to remove the garment he winced with pain.

'Here,' she said, 'let me help.' Gently she slid the shirt over his shoulders and he withdrew his arm on the injured side. Immediately she could see a large area of injury from his shoulder to the centre of his back, as if he'd been struck by something both heavy and sharp. The area was badly grazed and would, no doubt, have extensive bruising, while in its centre a deep gash looked as if it had bled profusely.

'What is it?' Dominic tried to peer over his shoulder. 'Tell me the worst.'

'Well, something obviously struck you,' said Claire. 'There's a gash a couple of inches long. It looks as if it's been bleeding a lot but it appears to have eased up now. I think you'll be black and blue tomorrow,' she added.

'Well, I don't think I've broken anything,' he replied. 'I can still use my arm, and my shoulder is OK, even if it does hurts like hell.' He pulled a face.

'You might have cracked a rib or two,' said Claire, 'and all this is because you were shielding me,' she added softly.

Slowly he turned and looked at her. 'Well, thank God it wasn't you,' he replied. For a long moment their eyes met, as once again they were both reminded how close to death they had been.

In the end Claire was forced to turn away, unable to face what she saw in his eyes. 'Let me try and clean you up,' she said huskily.

Without another word he turned his back to her again then lowered himself to the dusty floor where she knelt beside him and attempted to clean his wound. Fortunately the area, having been protected by his shirt, was fairly clean.

'Do you have a handkerchief?' she asked at last.

'Yes, somewhere.' He fumbled in one of his trouser pockets and produced a white handkerchief.

Carefully Claire folded the material into a pad then, untying the chiffon scarf that bound her hair, she shook her head, allowing her hair to fall loose—only too aware as she did so that Dominic was watching her closely. Positioning the pad over the wound, she secured it with the scarf, which she wound under Dominic's arm before tying it round his neck.

'I can't imagine that will be very comfortable,' she said with a grimace, 'but it's better than nothing and it should help to protect the wound.'

'Thank you, Nurse.' Momentarily there was a hint of amusement in his eyes and in spite of the seriousness of the situation Claire found herself smiling back. Then the tenderness of the moment was over and with a deep sigh Dominic hauled himself to his feet and allowed Claire to help him to put his shirt on again.

'I think, Nurse Schofield,' he said wryly as he fastened his buttons, 'it's time that you and I did a ward round.'

'Absolutely, Dr Hansford,' she replied, adopting the same wryly humorous tone as him. 'Otherwise our patients will be wondering what on earth has happened to us.'

CHAPTER FOUR

THE next hour was spent checking on those who had been injured, adjusting the improvised dressings and generally trying to make people as comfortable as possible with the very limited resources available. Ted continued to be in a great deal of pain, the paracetamol he had been given having barely touched the pain from his fractured leg. And while the bleeding from Peter's head wound seemed to have stopped, the same couldn't be said for Diane, whose wound continued to seep blood and who remained unconscious. Claire helped Russell to fashion another pad from his discarded shirt and then proceeded to hold it to the wound herself in an attempt to staunch the blood flow, while Dominic called an impromptu meeting of the others in order to take stock of their situation.

'It looks as if we could be here for some considerable time,' he said. 'What we need to do is to establish exactly what we have in the way of fluids and nourishment—by that I mean sweets, chewing gum, anything you might have—so, please, everyone, go through your pockets and your bags and see what you can find.'

Amidst much muttering and speculation the search revealed another can of soft drink which Dominic lined up alongside the can of Coke and the bottle of mineral water. Gradually people began to produce sweets from the depths of pockets and the corners of handbags.

'OK,' said Dominic at last, 'we have two packets of peppermints, half a dozen barley-sugar sweets and a couple of cereal bars. Oh, and two sticks of chewing gum. Not exactly a feast but there could well come a point when we'll be glad of them. Now…' he looked at the ring of silent faces around him '…there are eighteen of us in here. Most of us have received cuts and bruising, three have more serious injuries and one lady has a serious medical condition.'

'What about that man over there in the corner?' asked a woman whom Claire didn't recognise.

There was no easy way to say it. 'Unfortunately,' said Dominic, 'he didn't make it.' Amidst murmurings of shock and concern he went on, 'Does anyone know who he is?'

'I think he worked here.' It was the woman who had asked the question who answered. 'I'm sure it's the man who was standing behind the exhibits on the trestle tables when we first came in.'

'Poor fellow,' said Dominic. 'He took the full force of that huge section of roof as it caved in.'

In awe everyone looked up and Claire gave a shudder as she recalled that terrible moment and the noise the roof had made as it had collapsed.

'Fortunately he wouldn't have known anything about it,' said Dominic. 'I examined him shortly afterwards and he was already dead. I would say he died instantly. There was nothing to be done for him, but for the rest of us—we need to work out a plan of survival.'

'What do you mean?' demanded Melanie. 'You talk as if we're going to be here for ages.'

'Which we could well be,' said Archie with a shrug.

'Of course we won't,' said Melanie, and there was a note of hysteria in her voice now. 'I expect the emergency services are on their way right now.'

'They might not be,' someone else chipped in. 'We don't know what damage has been done elsewhere, do we? Buildings could have been destroyed in the town and people may have been trapped there as well.'

'Which is why we need to think out some sort of plan for ourselves,' said Dominic. 'I propose, and I'm sure you will all agree, that we save what little resources we have in case things get really desperate and even then precedence will be given to those who are badly injured or sick.'

There were nods and murmurings of agreement from those around them.

'In the meantime,' Dominic went on, 'I suggest those of us guys who are able-bodied should have another careful look to see if there isn't any other way out of here.'

'Just what I was thinking,' said Rob. 'And if there isn't, couldn't we start moving the rubble that's blocking the entrance?'

'Let's go and have a look,' said Dominic.

As some of the men made their way towards the entrance, which was practically hidden by the huge mound of rubble, Russell crouched down beside Claire and Diane again. 'How's the bleeding?' he asked, a note of desperation in his voice.

Claire gently lifted the pad and looked at it. 'I think,' she said after a moment, 'it's actually easing up a bit.'

'Do you?' asked Russell. 'Do you really?'

'Yes, I do,' Claire replied. 'Before, it was soaking through a pad immediately—it isn't doing that now. I'll put it back, then you take over, we need to keep up the pressure for a time.'

Russell changed places with her and continued to hold the pad torn from his shirt to the side of his wife's head. 'I don't know what I would do if I was to lose her,' he said. 'I can't imagine life without her.' His gaze flickered briefly towards Claire. 'I know we might not have come across as the most devoted of couples,' he said, 'but I really do love her.'

'I'm sure you do,' murmured Claire. 'Just as I'm sure she loves you.'

'Well, I hope so.' Russell gave a sigh. 'Actually, you

know, this trip to Rome was a last-ditch attempt to save our marriage.'

'Really?' said Claire feigning surprise. The last thing she wanted was for this poor man to suspect that there had been gossip amongst his companions about the state of his marriage.

'It was my fault, you know,' he went on after a moment. 'I nearly blew it. I had an affair, you see.'

Claire really didn't want to hear his confession but she knew from the counselling work that she did that it was probably vitally important for Russell at that particular moment to talk about what was troubling him.

'Would it help to talk about it?' she asked softly. 'It wouldn't go any further,' she added.

'Her name was Julie,' he said, 'she worked at the same company as me. She was half my age. I suppose I was flattered that a gorgeous-looking girl like her should even look at a silly old fool like me—but she did, and I fell for it. I thought I loved her—I couldn't think about anything else, she just took over my life. I didn't care about Diane or my kids.'

'So what happened?' asked Claire, leaning forward and picking up Diane's wrist to check her pulse. 'How did Diane find out?'

'I guess I became careless.' Russell shrugged. 'On the other hand, I think there was a part of me that almost wanted her to find out—you know, to force some sort of issue. I couldn't have gone on the way I was for much longer—the stress was killing me. Anyway, Di found out and issued me with an ultimatum—give up the girl or get out. I suppose I was lucky that she didn't chuck me out anyway.'

'So you ended the affair?' asked Claire.

He nodded. 'Yes, when I was finally faced with it, I couldn't leave. I suppose it was because of the kids really—

my son, Jamie, broke his heart, you see… But it was the hardest thing I've ever had to do. I wanted to keep phoning her and, I admit, to start with I did—a few times. But then I suppose I started to get over it and I tried, I tried really hard with Diane but, quite honestly, she didn't really want to know and if I'm honest it's been uphill all the way.'

'And the girl?' asked Claire.

'She met someone else—it nearly killed me when I heard about it from another colleague but I suppose I've got used to it. She's living with the guy now and they have a baby…'

'And you and Diane—how is it now?'

'It's been very hard going,' Russell admitted sadly. Looking down at his wife, he stretched out his other hand and tenderly smoothed a strand of hair back from her forehead. 'Sometimes she's been like a stranger to me, and at other times I find myself doubting she'll ever love me again…'

'And what about you, how do you feel about her?'

'I wasn't sure,' he admitted. 'That sounds dreadful, I know, but I really didn't know how I felt. I suppose I gave up Julie because of the kids, I don't know.' He shook his head. 'But to think it's taken something like this to prove to me what I really feel…and now, oh, God, it might be too late…'

'I'm sure she'll be all right,' said Claire gently. 'Hopefully we'll soon be able to get her to hospital.'

'I wish I could put the clock back,' said Russell, 'to how things were…before I met Julie.'

'Well, that may not be possible,' replied Claire. 'What you have to do is to build a new relationship with Diane, but you have to give her time to build her trust again. It isn't easy, but it can be done.' She paused. 'Tell me,' she said after a moment, 'whose idea was this holiday?'

'Diane's, actually,' he replied. 'She'd always wanted to

go to Rome and I went along with the idea because I thought it might help to improve things between us.'

'And has it?'

'Not really. We kept sniping at each other...'

'You may find that things will be different after this.'

'I hope so,' he said, his voice breaking with emotion. 'Oh, I do hope so.'

At that moment Dominic and Archie returned and Claire looked up questioningly. 'Any luck?' she said.

Dominic shook his head. 'No, it was too dangerous to start pulling the rubble away. If we had, there was a chance of the whole roof caving in.'

'It's the same with the other door,' said Archie. 'The pile of rubble behind that is enormous—the door won't move more than a couple of inches.'

'How's Diane?' Dominic crouched beside the injured woman.

'The bleeding seems to be easing up,' said Claire.

'Well, I think that's the only good piece of news we've had,' Dominic replied.

'Claire.' Rob was suddenly at her side. 'Could you have a word with Nicola for me?'

'Of course. Where is she?' Claire scrambled to her feet.

'Over here.' Rob led the way to where his young wife was sitting with her back to the wall. Her head was back and her eyes closed.

'Nicola?' Claire bent over the girl. 'What is it?'

Nicola's eyelids flickered then she looked up at Claire and for the briefest of moments Claire could see the fear in her eyes. Claire glanced up at Rob. 'Rob,' she said casually, 'could you just go and check on Ted for me, please?'

As Rob moved away Claire knelt beside Nicola. 'Are you going to tell me about it?' she said quietly.

'I'm scared,' said Nicola simply.

'We all are,' said Claire. 'That's nothing to be ashamed of.'

'No, you don't understand.' Nicola shook her head and Claire caught a glimpse of tiny beads of perspiration on her forehead.

'So what is this about?' she asked.

Nicola took a deep breath. 'Rob and me,' she said after a moment, 'we weren't due to get married until next year but then we brought it forward when I found I was pregnant. Oh, I know a lot of people don't worry about things like that these days,' she said quickly, 'but we wanted to do it properly…'

'How far on are you?' asked Claire.

'Just over twelve weeks,' Nicola replied. 'The thing is, I keep needing to go to the loo—I don't think I can wait much longer—and the other thing is that I've got some backache…'

'How long have you had that?' asked Claire urgently.

'Just in the last half-hour or so, but I don't want Rob to know—he's worried enough as it is.'

'Right,' said Claire, straightening up and looking round, 'first of all I think we need to find a private corner for you well away from everyone else. Then, if your backache persists, I'll ask Dominic to take a look at you.'

Some of the statues on the dais at the end of the room had been shattered while others had toppled over, but the sheer bulk of them at least offered Nicola the shelter and privacy she needed. When at last she emerged, Claire, who had waited for her, raised questioning eyebrows. 'Well?' she said.

'What a relief!' Nicola exclaimed. 'I thought I was going to burst.'

'Was there any bleeding?' asked Claire.

'No, thank God,' Nicola replied. 'I really was beginning to expect the worst.' Suddenly she giggled weakly.

'What is it?' Claire frowned.

'Do you think that could be called the protection of the saints?' Nicola looked over her shoulder at the heap of broken statues.

'It could well be.' Claire chuckled then, growing serious again, she said, 'I'd like you to go back to where you were and rest now. Try and find something so that you can raise your feet.'

'All right.' Nicola nodded. 'Thanks, Claire,' she added.

Claire watched as the girl slowly made her way back through the debris to her husband. She could still hardly believe that what had started as a pleasant day out had turned to this chaos, resulting in these life-and-death situations.

For the following hour or so Claire and Dominic continued to tend to the injured and the sick, carefully rationing out the fluids they had and calming and reassuring as best they could.

Once, briefly, Dominic touched her arm and Claire looked up to see an expression of tender concern in his brown eyes.

'What is it?' she asked in surprise.

'I just wondered if you were all right,' he said softly. 'You seem to be dashing around tending to everyone else—but what about you?'

'Oh, I'm OK,' Claire replied lightly, touched but at the same time embarrassed by his obvious concern. 'I'm one of the lucky ones.' What she didn't say was that her head had started to ache and the combination of the dust and the heat seemed to have brought on a raging thirst. 'How's your shoulder?' she asked, leaning sideways and glancing at the back of his shirt.

'It's all right.' He nodded then, looking round the vast room at the little groups of people amongst the debris and the rubble, he added, 'I was just wondering how much longer we will be able to keep everybody calm.'

'They seem OK at the moment,' Claire replied, then added. 'One thing I maybe should mention is that Nicola is twelve weeks pregnant.'

'Good grief.' Dominic threw her a sharp glance. 'Is she all right?'

'I hope so, although she was complaining of backache. I've told her to lie down with her feet raised.' She was silent for a moment. 'I can hardly believe the number of situations we are being faced with,' she said after a while.

'And there will be more, I fear,' said Dominic grimly. 'As people become dehydrated and hungry, we will start to have real problems on our hands.'

'Surely we will be rescued before then?' said Claire.

'Well, let's hope so,' Dominic replied. He paused. 'I keep listening,' he said after a moment, 'and I don't know if you've noticed, but there isn't a sound outside—it's almost as if we are the only ones left in the world.'

'I know.' Claire agreed. 'I thought the same. I keep hoping to hear the sound of sirens—but there's nothing—except for once, briefly I did hear birds singing.'

'Well, I suppose that's something,' said Dominic wryly. 'At least the world hasn't come to an end. I think I'll go and check on Ted. Will you have a look at Evelyn?'

As he turned away there came the sudden jangling tones of a mobile phone. The noise, like the chimes of an ice-cream van on a cold winter's day was so incongruous and unexpected that people looked up, sudden hope on their faces as Rob pressed a button and lifted the phone to his ear.

In the sudden silence everyone listened, straining to hear as Rob spoke briefly then listened before speaking again. As he pressed the button signalling the end of the conversation he looked around at the sea of anxious faces.

'Well?' demanded Melanie, her voice ragged with strain and emotion.

'That was my father,' said Rob.

'We didn't think it was a double-glazing salesman,' said Desmond with a snort.

'He phoned the police in the UK,' said Rob, ignoring Desmond, 'and reported our situation. They have now contacted the authorities in Assisi...'

'Well, thank God for that,' said Melanie. 'So they must be on their way by now.'

'We hope so,' replied Rob uneasily.

'What do you mean, "we hope so"?' Melanie's voice was beginning to rise again.

'What else did your father say, Rob?' asked Dominic calmly.

Rob took a deep breath. 'He said they were just getting reports from Italy on the television news.'

'And?' Dominic prompted, when Rob appeared to hesitate.

'He said that the reports stated that severe earth tremors had been reported in the central and north-eastern parts of Italy. Much structural damage had been reported.' Rob spoke as if relaying word for word what his father had told him. 'Resulting in some loss of life and leaving many injured and homeless.'

In the silence that followed Rob's words it was as if everyone was trying to take in what he had just said and what it might mean to them. In the end it was Desmond who put those thoughts into words.

'What you're saying, then,' he said slowly, his florid face gleaming with sweat, 'is that we aren't the only ones.'

'But at least they know we're up here!' cried Melanie. 'Don't they?' she demanded, looking round at the others, wild-eyed when no one immediately answered her.

In the end, predictably, it was Dominic who tried to allay

her fears. 'Yes,' he said in those same calm tones he had used throughout the ordeal, 'they do know where we are, even if Luisa and Guiseppe and the others haven't been able to contact anyone—the authorities now know that we are trapped in here.'

'Oh, God!' Melanie stared at him as if the awful truth had only just occurred to her. 'Are you saying that the others on the coach might all be dead?'

'Let's hope not,' Dominic replied, 'but they could be injured with no means of communication. At least now we know that some sort of help will be on the way. But what we still don't know is how long that help will take. In the meantime we have to remain calm. We have our own injured to care for…' He broke off as a sudden, but by now almost familiar rumbling sound filled the air.

'It's another one!' someone screamed.

'Take cover!' cried someone else.

People scattered, some falling to the ground, others clinging together. Russell stretched himself over the unconscious figure of his wife as if by doing so he could shield her from further harm, May wrapped her arms around Ted in a gesture of quiet resignation, and once again Claire found herself gathered into Dominic's arms before he pulled her to the floor, shielding her body with his own as they all waited for the inevitable crashing of masonry which had followed the previous onslaught.

As she lay there beneath Dominic Claire realised that the sheer terror she had experienced the last time was no longer there, that this time it was as if she was prepared to face whatever it was that was to happen to them and that by simply being with Dominic enabled her to do so. As the rumbling noise subsided there came a rushing sound from the far corner of the vast room as if some loose debris was falling from the roof, but it was nothing like the dreadful crashing sounds of the first time and in thc profound silence that followed Claire was aware of the beating of Dominic's heart—or maybe it was simply an echo of her own—as he held her closely against him.

They lay there together for what seemed like eternity until eventually Dominic cautiously moved, lifting his head to look round the room. 'I think,' he murmured at last against Claire's ear, 'that we may just have got away with it this time.'

He could have moved then, quite easily. He could have got up and helped Claire to her feet, but he didn't. Instead, he moved his body so that she wasn't taking his full weight but continued to lie there with his arms around her, holding her close. And Claire, for her part, was quite content to stay there as if simply by being protected by Dominic's arms could prevent any further harm, as if by lying there together they could somehow make all the fear and anxiety of their situation simply melt away.

'Are you all right?' he whispered at last, lifting his head slightly and looking into her face.

'Yes,' she whispered back, staring into the depths of his dark eyes and seeing herself reflected there.

'I think we got off lightly that time,' he said. Still he continued to hold her and still she let him, not even wanting to move, as if by doing so something would be destroyed—not material things like stone, wood and plaster but something intangible, something more fragile but nevertheless very real.

'D'you reckon that's it?' called Desmond suddenly, breaking the spell and hurtling them back to reality. 'Or d'you think there's more to come?'

Dominic moved then but Claire could sense his reluctance as he finally released her. She felt suddenly bereft and wanted to draw him back, to cling to him, to have him hold her again.

'It looks as if that might be it,' said Peter, 'at least for the time being, although it must have weakened the building even more. Let's just hope the whole lot doesn't cave in on us.'

'Is everyone all right?' called Dominic as he finally tore himself away from Claire and scrambled to his feet. There were nods and murmurs of assent from the others.

During the next couple of hours Claire and Dominic endeavoured to make the injured feel more comfortable. Ted was given a further two painkillers washed down with another mouthful of soft drink, likewise Peter, who complained of pain from his head injury. Diane remained unconscious but the bleeding from her head wound finally ceased, and when Claire discreetly questioned Nicola about her backache she was told that it had all but disappeared.

'It was probably caused by fluid retention,' Claire observed. 'Don't let it build up again, will you? I know it's undignified but unfortunately we are all having to come to terms with it.' Some of the men had cordoned off a far corner of the room with the remains of the statues and the trestle tables to serve as latrines.

'The smell will become unbearable,' Melanie complained.

'I'm more concerned about the smell from the body,' said Dominic grimly. 'That really could pose a health hazard if we are here for any real length of time.'

'The other big worry is the shortage of drinking water,' said May.

At one point Claire looked up at the patch of sky that was visible through the broken roof and realised that it had darkened as dusk approached.

'Looks like we could be here for the night,' said Archie, who had followed her gaze.

'Oh, no,' moaned Nicola softly. 'Surely they will get here before it gets dark.'

'Well, if they don't, I can't see them getting rescue vehicles and equipment up here afterwards,' said Archie.

'You're right.' Dominic nodded then, raising his voice so that everyone could hear he said, 'We need to prepare ourselves in case we have to be here all night. There's no electric power so we won't have any lights. What I suggest is that while we still have daylight we make ourselves as comfortable as possible. Claire and I will pass round the cans of drink and everyone is to take a mouthful—the mineral water I will keep until the morning. We will also share out the sweets. Two each to everyone and, again, if there are any over, we will save them until the morning.'

Together Dominic and Claire moved from group to group, from person to person, passing round the few meagre but precious supplies and at the same time once again checking on the injured while daylight lasted.

'Is Evelyn all right?' Claire asked Dorothy as she crouched down beside the two women.

'I think so.' Dorothy cast an anxious glance towards her sister who lay propped against the wall, ashen-faced and with her eyes closed.

'Let me give her a sip of drink,' said Claire, leaning forward. 'Evelyn,' she said gently, 'take a sip.' She watched as the woman took a mouthful, hating herself when, as Evelyn would have taken more, she had to withdraw the can.

'Here, Dorothy,' she said. 'You have a sip as well.'

Dorothy shook her head. 'Give it to Evelyn.'

'No.' Claire held out the can. 'Dominic was insistent that everyone has a mouthful.'

'Very well.' Dorothy took the can and took a mouthful of the fizzy orange drink, swirling it around her mouth, savouring it, before swallowing it. 'Thank you,' she murmured at last, handing the can back to Claire. 'Tell me,' she said, 'what did that young man say about us being rescued? My hearing isn't very good these days.'

Briefly Claire outlined what Rob had told them.

'So it looks as if we could be here for the night,' said Dorothy when she had finished.

'Yes,' Claire agreed, 'it does seem that way. But try not to worry—I'm sure Evelyn will be all right.'

'I'm just thankful we have you with us,' Dorothy replied. 'You, and your husband, of course.'

'My husband?' Claire had been about to move away but at Dorothy's words she turned and stared at her.

'Yes,' Dorothy replied, 'the doctor. Dominic…'

'He isn't my husband,' said Claire quickly.

'Isn't he?' Dorothy looked amazed. 'I thought he was.'

'No, we'd never met each other until this trip.'

'Well, you do surprise me.' Dorothy shook her head. 'You seem like the perfect couple—I really took you for husband and wife—but, there, I always did think that God moves in mysterious ways, especially in the way he brings people together.' She smiled. 'But who would have thought he would use an earthquake to do it?'

CHAPTER FIVE

IT WAS a strange night—one that Claire would never forget as long as she lived—a night of restless mutterings and murmurings, of whispers and soft moans, a night of inky blackness relieved only by the strip of sky visible through the gaping hole in the roof and a night which, after the intense heat of the day, quickly grew cold in the stone-floored, austere monastery building. No one had anything by way of covering so people were forced to huddle together for warmth. By the time that Claire and Dominic had finished checking on the injured and had found a corner in which to try to sleep, it seemed the most natural thing in the world for Dominic to sit against the wall and to draw Claire into his arms so that she could lay her head against his shoulder and so that they each could draw warmth from the other.

She dozed fitfully, awaking when Dominic stirred.

'I need to check on Diane and Ted,' he whispered.

'I'll take a look at Evelyn,' she replied, shaking her head and trying to recover her bearings. As quietly as they could, in order not to disturb anyone who might be sleeping, Dominic and Claire carried out their night round of those who were injured or sick. Claire found Evelyn sleeping, watched over by Dorothy.

'Try and get some rest yourself,' she said to Dorothy in a low voice. On her way back to her corner she checked briefly on Nicola and Rob. Rob appeared to be asleep but Nicola was awake. 'Are you all right?' whispered Claire.

'Yes, I think so,' Nicola replied softly. 'I was just psyching myself up to go to the loo again.'

'No backache?' asked Claire.

'No, not this time.' Gently extricating herself from her husband's protecting arm, Nicola climbed stiffly to her feet.

Claire took her hand. 'Come on,' she said. 'I'll go with you. I don't want you tripping over—a fall is the last thing you need at the moment.'

When Claire eventually returned to her corner, after making sure Nicola was safely back with her husband, she found that Dominic had returned. 'Everything all right?' she asked softly.

'Yes. Ted was very uncomfortable so I gave him two more paracetamol—they were the only two left. Heaven knows what he'll do in the morning, poor man.'

'And Diane?' asked Claire.

'She's in a bad way,' replied Dominic. 'She's in a coma—she needs an infusion and to be catheterised. Russell is marvellous with her but...' He trailed off, his unspoken words summing up his concern.

'Let's just hope the rescue team gets through soon,' said Claire.

'If they don't, I fear we will lose Diane.' Dominic paused. 'What about Evelyn?'

'Sleeping, thankfully,' Claire replied, 'and I checked on Nicola—she seems to be OK. How about you?' she added softly. 'How's your shoulder?'

'It throbs like hell,' Dominic admitted ruefully, 'and my stomach must think my throat has been cut, judging by the noises it's making.'

'I know,' whispered Claire with a giggle as she settled down once again with her head on Dominic's good shoulder, 'I didn't believe I could be so hungry and still be alive. I only had yoghurt for breakfast this morning, I wish now I'd had everything that was going.'

'Don't talk about yoghurt,' said Dominic. 'I could devour a gallon right now and I don't even like the stuff that much.' He sighed, and tightening his grip around her, said, 'Try and get a bit more sleep.'

Dutifully she closed her eyes but this time she found it much more difficult to drop off for her brain seemed suddenly very active with dozens of totally unrelated thoughts teeming around and jostling for position. One moment she was thinking about her childhood in Hampshire, a carefree happy time where she had been the beloved only child and which had continued until her late teens when her mother had been stricken with breast cancer and had died, leaving Claire and her father bereft and desolate. She thought about her nursing training and the friends she had made, the jobs that had followed, in various hospitals in the south of England and finally her job at the Hargreaves Centre. She thought about Mike and how bizarre it was that she should be thinking of him while lying in the arms of another man.

In that darkest of hours just before dawn Claire abandoned all ideas of sleep as once again she and Dominic checked on the sick, helping May and Russell to cope as they in turn struggled to help their spouses. But later, when they returned to snatch maybe an hour of rest, she finally must have slept for when she next stirred and opened her eyes it was to daylight and blue sky beyond the gaping hole in the roof, together with the ever optimistic song of the birds in what once had been the monastery garden.

Turning her head, she realised she was alone, that somehow Dominic had moved without waking her. Sitting up, she stretched and yawned, rubbing her eyes, easing her aching limbs before finally, with a deep sigh, hauling herself to her feet. Trying to ignore or stifle the clamouring of her own body's needs, she made her way across the floor to see what help she could give.

She found Dominic at Diane's side, moistening her mouth with a little of the precious mineral water. After helping Russell to cope as best he could, they went next to

Ted, then to Peter, Evelyn, Nicola and the others. The water ran out before they were halfway round, likewise the sweets that were left and the small pieces of cereal bars—not enough to go round, with Dominic, Archie, Desmond and Rob receiving nothing. Claire had refused her portion but Dominic had insisted she take it and in the end she had been forced to take her mouthful of water and a boiled barley sugar sweet. She had never known anything to taste so good and she kept the sweet in her mouth until it was barely more than a sliver when what she really wanted to do was suck it away immediately and let the juices trickle down her parched throat.

At eight o'clock Rob's father phoned again but Rob was only able to tell him that they were still waiting for the emergency services and that for some of them the situation was becoming crucial when the battery on his mobile phone ran out and their last link with the outside world was severed.

'I meant to charge it before we left the hotel,' said Rob apologetically, looking helplessly round at the others, 'but I was a bit late and I thought I might miss the coach so I thought I'd leave it until I got back.'

'I bet you wish you *had* missed the coach now,' said Desmond. Even his voice was dulled now and as Diane's condition continued to deteriorate and Ted's pain worsened a sense of despair began to creep over the group and settle like mist over marshland.

It was late morning when Claire saw Dominic lift his head and appear to listen.

'What is it?' She held her breath, listening herself for that ominous rumbling sound. 'Is it another tremor?' she whispered in dread.

'No.' Dominic shook his head then, glancing at Archie who also had lifted his head and was listening, he said, 'Can you hear it as well?'

'Yes.' Archie nodded then scrambled to his feet. 'It's a siren. I would say it's some way off, but it's definitely a siren.'

'Oh, thank God!' cried Melanie. 'We're going to be rescued.'

A ripple of relief and expectation ran through the room as people hugged each other and someone burst into tears.

It was a further hour, however, before they could hear sounds of activity outside.

'It's going to take some while before they clear through the rubble to get in to us,' warned Dominic as people began preparing themselves to leave.

'Maybe,' said Claire, 'but at least something is happening.'

'Not a moment too soon for Diane,' said Dominic in a low voice. 'She's not good this morning.'

'She survived the night,' replied Claire softly. 'There was a moment when I doubted she would do that.'

Within an hour all that could be heard were the sounds of digging as a rescue team hacked its way from the cloisters into the vast room. At one point when all suddenly went quiet it was possible to communicate verbally with their rescuers, although what was actually said was very limited as no one's Italian was up to much, and the rescuers appeared to be in possession of no English.

And then, just as spirits were raised and optimism was soaring at the prospect of imminent rescue, there came a sudden cry of alarm from Dorothy.

'Oh, quickly, quickly, it's Evelyn! Come quickly. Doctor!'

Within seconds both Dominic and Claire were by Evelyn's side. Propped against the wall, she appeared ashen-faced and her hands were clutching at her chest then she seemed to give a huge sigh before slumping sideways.

Dominic leaned over her. 'She's arrested,' he said

calmly. 'Lay her down—that's right. Her airways are clear. Good. Come on, Claire, we'll resuscitate together. I'll start cardiac massage—you breathe.'

Together Claire and Dominic instinctively fell into the rhythm of resuscitation, with Dominic administering five sharp thumps to the left side of Evelyn's chest with the ball of his linked hands then Claire pinching Evelyn's nose and giving a breath into her mouth.

They continued with this routine, watched by Dorothy, Melanie and Archie, for what seemed like hours but which, in reality, could have only been for a few minutes until, at last, they paused and Dominic checked Evelyn's pulse.

'Nothing,' he said. 'Again,' he added, and they resumed the procedure while Dorothy wrung her hands in anguish as she stood by helplessly and watched as the two medics fought for her sister's life.

Just when it would have appeared to any of the onlookers that all was lost, Dominic stopped the massage. 'We have an output—she's breathing,' he said with a grunt of satisfaction while Claire sat back on her heels with a huge sigh of relief.

'Oh, thank you, thank you,' wept Dorothy, who by this time was completely overcome by emotion.

'Try and keep her warm,' said Dominic. 'Hopefully, soon now we'll be able to get her to hospital.'

Even as he spoke there came a triumphant shout from the far end of the room as, to the cheers of those inside, the first of the rescuers broke through.

Because of the painstaking nature of the work, however, which involved the careful removal of the rubble and the constant fear of further collapse, it was a further two hours before the debris could be sufficiently cleared to allow access.

But at last an Italian medical team gained entry and after difficult consultation with Dominic and Claire administered first aid to the injured. Oxygen was given to Evelyn and Diane and infusions set up for Diane and Ted, and within the next hour the injured were carried on stretchers out of the refectory, through the cloisters and into waiting ambulances.

The rest of the group, dishevelled and exhausted, including Dominic and Claire, were taken to a minibus where it was explained to them that they were also to be taken to hospital in nearby Assisi to be checked over. As they finally drove away from the hilltop monastery Claire allowed herself a backward glance at the ancient building which for all those hours had been their prison and which at times had threatened to become their tomb.

From outside it was possible to see the extent of the damage, from the huge section of missing roof to the ominous cracks which had appeared in the walls and which had split large sections of the ground around the monastery.

'We're lucky to be alive,' said Dominic, voicing what everyone must have been thinking. As they left the monastery behind an attendant issued everyone with bottles of water, and as they drank, slaking their overwhelming thirst, they one by one fell silent as the extent of the damage caused by the earth tremors became apparent.

Villages that they travelled through had been badly hit with houses destroyed, leaving bewildered people who now stood in shocked groups or trying to collect their possessions and the shattered remnants of their lives. Of the coach they had travelled in to the monastery there was no sign.

'Let's hope they got away,' said Desmond at last, speaking for them all.

They remained silent after that as they sped towards Assisi, and when Claire felt Dominic take her hand she was content for him to do so, letting her head fall onto his shoulder as a sudden, overwhelming sense of fatigue crept over her.

The next few hours were to become a blur in Claire's mind—their arrival at the hospital, being checked over by medical staff, Claire being treated for mild delayed shock and Dominic having his wound dressed, being given a meal and hot drinks then finally visiting those of their party who had been admitted.

Diane had been taken directly to the hospital's high-dependency unit and they found her surrounded by high-tech equipment with Russell by her side.

'She's in good hands now, Russell,' said Dominic.

'She's been in good hands all along,' replied Russell huskily. 'I'll never be able to thank you two enough for all you've done for her. They are going to give her a scan tomorrow so I'll know more then about her condition.'

'Keep in touch, won't you?' said Claire. 'We want to know how she gets on.'

'Of course.' Russell nodded before turning back to the still figure of his wife.

Evelyn had been admitted to the cardiac unit and was being closely monitored. Dorothy was quite tearful when she said goodbye to Dominic and Claire. 'We are going to arrange a flight home just as soon as Evelyn can be moved,' she said, 'but I know when all this is over Evelyn will want to thank the two of you herself.'

'That's not necessary,' said Dominic gently.

'You saved her life,' replied Dorothy. 'If it wasn't for you, she wouldn't be here now.'

They found Ted in the emergency department, awaiting a transfer to the hospital's orthopaedic unit to have surgery to set his shattered thigh.

'They said if it wasn't for these splints I could have been looking at the rest of my life in a wheelchair,' he said, looking at Dominic as he spoke.

'Are you sure you understood that correctly?' asked

Dominic with a weary smile. 'I don't think my Italian would have been up to that.'

'Ah,' said May, who was sitting beside her husband, 'this doctor spoke very good English. He said those table legs saved the day.'

'In that case, it should be Archie you should be thanking.'

May smiled but from the look she gave Claire it was obvious where she thought their true gratitude lay.

Peter was to be kept in overnight with suspected concussion, and Nicola was also to stay overnight just as a precautionary measure in view of her pregnancy, but it was finally agreed that, with the exception of the spouses or partners of the injured who would be accommodated locally, the others would be taken back to their hotels in Rome.

Gradually they began to piece together the wider picture and greater effects of the earth tremors. Confirming what Rob's father had told them, Archie and Desmond found out that a fairly large area had been affected in central and north-eastern Italy, resulting in much structural damage. The hospital to which they had been taken had been on full red alert and had been inundated with casualties from the nearby villages.

'Did you manage to find out anything about Luisa and Guiseppe and the others?' asked Claire anxiously as they sat in the hospital foyer, awaiting transport.

'Yes,' Archie replied. 'Apparently the coach was badly damaged after an outer wall of the monastery collapsed on it. There were several injuries as there were still people sitting in the coach. The injured were brought to this hospital but as far as I can make out they have all been released and have been taken back to Rome.'

It was a very subdued and exhausted group on the drive back to Rome, a far cry from the high-spirited, expectant band who had set out forty-eight hours before on their ill-fated trip to Assisi.

On their arrival at the hotel Claire went straight to her room where she collapsed onto her bed and slept for eight solid hours.

When she finally awoke she couldn't at first think where she was or what had happened to her, but as she lay on her back and gazed at patterns of sunlight on the ceiling it slowly flooded over her as she recalled all that had happened.

Turning her head, she looked at her bedroom clock and saw that it was five o'clock in the afternoon. She lay there for a time collecting her thoughts, until at last with a sigh she sat up, winced when she realised she ached all over then gingerly swung her legs to the floor and stood up. For one dreadful moment the room seemed to lurch and sway. She closed her eyes and when she reopened them was relieved to find that everything seemed to have returned to normal. Slowly she padded across the floor to the shower room and allowed herself the sheer bliss of standing beneath the jet of water as it washed away all outward traces of the ordeal of the past two days. The inward effects, she suspected, would take longer to disappear. She wondered about Dominic, whether he was awake and if his shoulder was giving him pain. Maybe, she thought, when she was dressed she would phone his room.

She had just finished drying her hair when her phone rang, and because she had been thinking about Dominic she imagined it would be him. 'Hello?' she said eagerly on lifting the receiver.

'There is a call for you,' said a voice with a very strong Italian accent. 'I put you through.'

Still she thought it would be Dominic. 'Hello?' she said again.

'Hello?' said another voice, a very English voice this

time, a voice that was instantly recognisable and so familiar but which because of recent events seemed to belong to another totally different existence, 'It's me, Mike.'

'Oh, Mike!' She swallowed. She'd completely forgotten about Mike.

'Claire, are you all right?' he said. 'I've been trying to ring your mobile but I haven't been able to get through.'

'Yes, I'm all right,' she replied. Suddenly she felt weak just standing there and sank down onto the bed.

'We heard reports of the earth tremors,' said Mike. 'I wasn't too worried at first because I knew you were in Rome—nowhere near the tremors—but then when I couldn't reach you on your mobile I rang the hotel… You *are* all right, aren't you, darling?'

'Well, I am now,' Claire replied weakly.

'What do you mean? Rome wasn't affected, was it?'

'No, but I wasn't in Rome.'

'Where were you, then?' he demanded.

'We were on an excursion to Assisi—I did tell you we were going, Mike.'

'Did you? I don't remember.'

No, she thought, because you were too concerned about Emma's exams at the time. 'Well, I did,' she said. 'Anyway, we rather got caught up in things.'

'But you are all right now?'

'Yes…yes, I'm all right now.' She was about to tell him that others in her party had been seriously injured, that someone had been killed, about the terror and the anguish of it all, but he gave her no chance.

'Well, thank God for that,' he said. 'I'm still not sure I should have let you go without me. Anyway, you'll have to tell me all about it when you get home. Emma wants to pick your brains as well—she's doing a project on ancient Rome. But talking of coming home—in view of this earthquake business, will you be coming any earlier?'

Claire found herself gripping the receiver a little tighter then heard herself say, 'No, I shouldn't think so, Mike. I'll see you on Saturday as arranged.'

'All right,' he said. 'I'm afraid I won't be able to get to the airport to pick you up—I'm on call—but take care, won't you?'

'Yes, I will— Oh, Mike,' she said, 'just one thing. Would you ring my father for me and tell him I'm all right, just in case he's been worrying?'

'Will do. Bye, my love. I love you.'

'Bye, Mike,' she said slowly. 'I love you, too,' she added automatically.

She found Dominic half an hour later sitting at a table on the hotel terrace with a glass of beer in front of him. He stood up as she walked towards him and pulled out a chair so she could join him.

'Hello,' he said softly, and as his gaze met hers her heart turned over. 'I was just coming to look for you,' he added. As she sat down he raised one hand to summon the ever-attentive waiter who hovered nearby. 'What would you like?' he asked.

'Just iced water, please,' she replied.

'Are you all right?' he asked, his voice suddenly full of concern, 'I was getting worried about you.'

'Were you?' A faint smile touched her mouth and as she looked at him she noticed that he still looked tired and rather drawn. 'I slept much longer than I intended.'

'That's good,' he said. 'You needed it.'

'What about you?' she asked. 'Did you sleep?'

'Not very well,' he admitted.

'Your shoulder—was it painful?'

'A bit, ' he admitted, 'but it wasn't really that—it was more that my brain decided to run an action replay of the last forty-eight hours.'

'It's terrible when that happens,' said Claire looking up, shielding her eyes from the early evening sun and smiling at the waiter as he arrived with a tray bearing a glass and a jug of iced water, 'but you'll probably sleep well tonight, while my body clock will be completely out of sync.' She paused and looked around at the masses of flowers and the cypress trees that fringed the terrace and whose shadows across the flagstones were growing longer as the sun sank slowly behind the distant hills. 'Have you seen any of the others?' she asked after a moment.

'A few of them were around earlier,' he replied. 'Desmond and Archie and a couple of the others.'

'Did they say what they are going to do?'

'The general feeling seems to be to get flights home as soon as they can.'

'I can understand that,' said Claire thoughtfully as she sipped her drink. 'What about Archie—is he going home?'

'No, but I understand he was moving on tomorrow anyway.' Dominic paused. 'What will you do, Claire?' He spoke casually, throwing her a sidelong glance.

'I'm not sure,' she admitted. 'There's a part of me that longs for home but...on the other hand it might be nice just to stay here and rest for a while. After all, it's only until Saturday—I was going then anyway.' She was silent again then, looking at Dominic from under her lashes, said, 'How about you?'

'I was going at the weekend as well,' he replied, still in the same casual tones. 'I'd planned to move on to Austria and then to Prague for a couple of days.'

'Will you still do that?' she asked.

'Yes, I think so.' He nodded. 'You can't let something like an earthquake put paid to all your plans.'

'No, of course not,' she agreed with a smile.

'In which case,' he went on smoothly, not looking at her but instead appearing to intently scrutinise his glass and the remainder of his drink, 'I suggest we make the most of our last couple of days in Rome in this rather lovely old hotel. What do you say?'

'I think,' she said, ignoring the warning bell that was sounding somewhere at the back of her brain, 'that sounds like a very good idea.'

CHAPTER SIX

DURING the next twenty-four hours Claire and Dominic slept, ate, slept some more and generally recuperated from their ordeal, much of the time lying side by side on sunbeds on the hotel terrace. At first they were mostly silent as they came to terms with all that had happened, but very gradually the need to talk crept in and they found themselves going over the devastating series of events. At times they questioned the course of action they had taken, wondering if they could have done more or if what they had done should have differed in any way. Diane's name was the one that came up most frequently as they agonised over how little they had actually been able to do for her.

'I'll phone Assisi later,' said Dominic, looking at his watch at one point during the afternoon, 'and see whether they have the results of her scan.' He paused and looked at Claire over the top of his sunglasses. 'Have you spoken to your doctor?' he asked suddenly.

She wanted to protest to say Mike *wasn't* her doctor, but decided that would sound ridiculous, because to all intents and purposes he was her doctor, at least that was the way it would seem to Dominic. 'He phoned, soon after we got back,' she said.

'He must have been out of his mind with worry.' Dominic leaned back on his sunbed, his hands behind his head. 'I know I would have been.'

When Claire remained silent he lifted his head and looked at her. 'Well,' he said, 'wasn't he?'

'Actually, no,' she admitted. 'You see,' she hastened to explain when she saw his expression begin to change, 'although he'd obviously heard about the earth tremors, he'd thought I was here in Rome…'

'So you hadn't told him about the proposed trip to Assisi?' Dominic's tone changed slightly.

'Well, yes, I did as it happens,' Claire replied slowly, 'but I don't think he could have taken it in because he didn't appear to be concerned in any way.'

Dominic had lowered his arms now and was staring at her, but because of the sunglasses she wasn't able to see the expression in his eyes. Suddenly she was glad of that for she had a feeling that what she might see there would make her feel uncomfortable. 'I hope,' he said at last, 'that you put him straight over that matter.'

'Well—' she began, but he carried on, not giving her time for excuses.

'That you were in the thick of it, that you could have been killed along with your companions. That people were seriously injured,' he went on relentlessly, 'that a man died… You did tell him those things?'

Hearing a note of incredulity creeping into his tone, Claire took a deep breath, 'Actually,' she said, 'no, I didn't.'

'So what did you tell him?' he demanded quietly.

She hesitated. 'That I got a bit caught up in things because I'd been travelling to Assisi and hadn't been here in Rome as he'd thought,' she said at last. 'But I then told him that I was all right and that he wasn't to worry.'

'And did he not want to know to what extent you were caught up in things?' That note of disbelief was back in Dominic's voice.

'Not really.' Claire shook her head. 'I think he was just relieved that I was all right. I told him I would tell him all about it when I get home.'

Dominic was silent but it was a tense silence and Claire

could feel the tautness of his body beside her almost as if they were touching.

'So why didn't you tell him?' he asked after a long silence.

'I don't know really.' She shrugged. 'I'm not sure...' She trailed off, uncertain how to continue. She did know really. It was because she knew that if she'd spelt things out to Mike he would have insisted that she come home immediately and somehow, in spite of everything, she hadn't wanted to do that.

Almost as if he could read her thoughts, Dominic said, 'Did he suggest you go home early?'

'No.' Claire shook her head. 'Although I suspect he might have done if he'd known the extent of things,' she admitted.

'But you didn't feel you wanted to get an earlier flight?' he asked softly.

'No, I didn't.' She was even more grateful now for the fact that she couldn't see his expression. 'I thought...I thought I needed a bit of time to get over everything...' she explained.

She was saved from further discussion by the sudden arrival of Melanie and Peter, and Nicola and Rob, who had returned to the hotel by coach after Peter's and Nicola's discharge from the hospital in Assisi. Hotel staff had obviously told them that Claire and Dominic were resting on the terrace and they had come to find them.

'Is everything all right?' asked Claire, looking from one to the other of them after she and Dominic had risen to their feet and they had all greeted each other with hugs and handshakes, for all the world like old friends meeting after a long period apart instead of people who hadn't even known one another the previous week.

'Yes.' Melanie nodded and speaking for Peter, who seemed uncharacteristically subdued, said, 'He has a bit of concussion and we have to report to our GP as soon as we get home but otherwise he's OK, aren't you, love?'

Peter nodded wearily. 'I just want to get home now,' he said. 'The tour rep has managed to get all four of us on a flight later tonight.' He glanced at Nicola and Rob as he spoke.

'Well, that's good.' Claire looked at Nicola and as Dominic and Peter began discussing flight details she said, 'Is everything all right, Nicola?'

'Yes, fine, thanks.' Nicola looked exhausted but appeared relieved that all was well with her pregnancy. 'They were wonderful at the hospital,' she said. 'They did an ultrasound scan and all is well. Like Peter, I have to report to my doctor when I get back to the UK.'

'Any news on Diane?' asked Dominic.

'No, nothing new,' Melanie replied. 'She was about to have a scan when we left.'

'I'll phone the hospital later and see if they have any results,' said Dominic.

'Aren't you going home?' asked Melanie curiously.

'Not yet,' replied Dominic lightly. 'We thought we'd leave any spare seats on UK-bound aircraft for those who really needed them, didn't we, Claire?'

'That's very noble of you,' said Peter, 'but we didn't have any trouble getting seats. I'm sure if you really wanted to go…'

'Maybe they don't want to,' said Melanie with a speculative glance from under her lashes at Claire and Dominic.

'What?' Peter frowned then as Melanie nudged him he said, 'Oh, I see. Oh, well, I guess that's up to you. Me? I can't wait to get home.'

'That's understandable,' said Dominic smoothly, 'especially for those who were injured.'

'But you were injured, weren't you?' said Nicola suddenly. 'Didn't I see Claire dressing a wound on your back?'

'Just a scratch.' Dominic shrugged.

'It was a bit more than that,' said Claire. 'They dressed it at the hospital...'

'Not enough to make me cut short my holiday,' said Dominic.

'But what about you, Claire?' asked Nicola anxiously.

'Oh,' said Claire. 'I wasn't injured, thanks to Dominic, so I thought I would relax also for a couple more days before going home.'

The little group broke up after that with Melanie and Peter and Nicola and Rob going off to their rooms to pack, leaving Claire and Dominic on the terrace to enjoy the last of the day's sunshine.

But later when Melanie called by Claire's room to say goodbye it was obvious she was more than curious as to what was happening.

'Do I smell romance in the air?' she asked.

'No, of course not,' Claire denied, only too aware that her face had flushed like a teenager's at the directness of Melanie's question.

'But you seem so right together,' said Melanie, inadvertently echoing Dorothy's words.

'Maybe it appears that way,' said Claire with a shrug, which she hoped appeared casual, 'but I can assure you it isn't the case. I am already in a relationship at home.'

'Oh, really?' Melanie sounded disappointed. 'Is it serious?'

'Yes, I think so.'

'You don't sound too sure.' Melanie raised one eyebrow.

'Oh, I am. Of course I am,' Claire replied firmly. 'Mike and I have been seeing each other for some time now... We work together...' She trailed off, suddenly aware that it sounded as if she was trying just a little too hard to explain her relationship with Mike.

'Well,' Melanie sighed, 'if he's the right one, my advice

to you would be to do something about it. Look at Peter and me,' she added. 'We've been living together for years and have never got around to getting married. Never thought we needed to. It's taken something like this to make us realise that we do want to be married—that we want the world to recognise us as a married couple, not just as two people who share a home.'

'You mean…?' Claire stared at her.

'Yes.' Melanie nodded. 'We are going to get married just as soon as it can be arranged.'

'Oh, Melanie, that's wonderful.' Stepping forward, Claire gave her a hug. 'I'm so pleased for you.'

'So all I'm saying,' said Melanie, 'is that if your Mike is the one then get on and do something about it…' She paused and looked searchingly at Claire. 'But on the other hand, if he isn't, then it's probably time to move on.'

Later, after the others had departed for the airport, Claire took a long bath and found herself thinking over the conversation she'd had with Melanie. She knew that Melanie and probably some of the others were thinking that there was something between herself and Dominic. That was the reason she had felt compelled to set the matter straight by telling Melanie that she was already involved in another relationship.

Even Dorothy had thought that she and Dominic were an item—no, more than that, she corrected herself, Dorothy had thought they were husband and wife. Claire found herself shifting her position slightly in the scented water, disturbed and somehow excited at the very thought. What if she hadn't been in a relationship with Mike? Would anything have evolved between herself and Dominic? Deep in her heart she had the feeling that it would have for she had been aware of that spark of attraction between them from the very moment they had set eyes on each other. And later, bizarre as the circumstances had been, when he had held her deep in the night in the chill of the old monastery building, she had been only too aware of the chemistry between them.

But what had Dominic's feelings been? It was too easy to say that if it wasn't for Mike something may have developed between them, because if it had, it may well have only been for the duration of the holiday. By his own admission Dominic was something of a drifter whose previous relationships with women had been jeopardised by the nature of his work. There was nothing to suggest that a relationship with her would prove to be any different.

So would she have settled for what essentially would have been a holiday romance—albeit with a twist? she asked herself.

No, her head told her, of course not. That sort of thing more often than not led to false expectations and even heartbreak and, besides, she'd never in her life gone in for a one-night stand or even a no-strings-attached affair.

Yes, her heart contradicted, just for once she would have thrown caution to the winds and enjoyed a brief fling with this intriguing, exciting man.

As the realisation hit her that that was what she would have done, deep inside she felt a little knot of desire and for a while she allowed herself to fantasise what it might be like to have him make love to her, running her hands over her wet body and pretending it was Dominic who was doing so.

By the time, reluctantly, she stirred and roused herself from the delights of her fantasy it was to find that the water had grown quite cold.

She dressed with care, choosing a red dress in a silky material with a low back and slender shoulder straps and brushing her hair so that it caressed her shoulders like a honey-coloured curtain. Later when she joined Dominic in the bar the admiration in his eyes caused her heart to beat faster. With his hand beneath her elbow they made their way to the hotel dining room, its windows flung wide tonight onto the terrace and the soft, balmy Italian night beyond where a new moon hung in the sky like a golden sickle and the air was motionless but heady with the scent of jasmine. But, and maybe because of the sheer indulgence of her recent thoughts, Claire found herself apprehensive in his presence.

'I phoned Assisi,' he said after they had ordered and the waiter had brought wine to their table.

She raised her eyebrows. 'Any news?'

'Diane's scan revealed a blood clot.'

'Oh, Dominic.' She stared at him in dismay.

'Hopefully they'll be able to disperse it,' he said, but his expression betrayed his doubt and concern.

She remained silent for a while, thinking of Diane and of Russell and of all he had told her about their marriage. 'Any news on the others?' she asked at last. 'Evelyn or Ted?'

'Evelyn is to be discharged tomorrow,' Dominic replied, 'and she and Dorothy are apparently flying home. Ted has had his operation and is comfortable.' He paused then, lifting his wineglass, he went on, 'Seeing today is his and May's wedding anniversary, I think we should drink a toast to them.'

'Of course.' Claire lifted her own glass.

'Ted and May,' said Dominic.

'Ted and May,' she echoed, but the moment was somehow bitter-sweet and Claire found herself picturing Ted and May and how happy they had been in looking forward to their golden wedding anniversary. If everything had gone according to plan, they would have all been celebrating together that very night, instead of which she and Dominic were in the hotel on their own, Ted and May were in Assisi and the others were scattered near and far.

'What will you do,' she heard herself say after a while, 'when you get home?' She wasn't sure why she asked but again knew it probably had something to do with the dangerous fantasising she had indulged in and the need to know what the future might hold for him.

'My contract at the hospital is finished,' he replied.

'So what next?' she asked, almost knowing what his answer would be.

'Provided my father is better, I guess I will go abroad again,' he replied slowly, studying the contents of his wineglass as he did so. 'One of the charities I work with was recruiting medical staff for an area hit by famine in Africa.'

'Oh,' she said with a little sigh. 'Yes, I see.'

'And what about you?' he asked a little later. He had been about to take a mouthful of food but he paused the fork halfway to his mouth, his steady gaze meeting hers across the table.

'Me?' she asked, playing for time.

'Yes, what will you do?' Not allowing her time to reply, he went on, 'Will you return to your work at the Hargreaves Centre and your life with your doctor friend?'

'Yes,' she said, 'yes, I suppose so.'

'You don't sound too sure.'

'Oh, I am. I will do that, of course I will.' She hesitated. 'It's just that I think after all that has happened I will find it very difficult getting back to normal…'

'In what respect,' he asked quietly, 'the job or the private life?'

'Both, I think,' she replied honestly.

Dominic was silent for a long moment. 'I think,' he said at last, 'that if you speak to anyone that has been through an experience such as we have that involved any sort of life-and-death situation they will say the same thing, that afterwards it is incredibly difficult to pick up the pieces of your life and get back to normality.'

'What about you?' she asked. 'Will you find it difficult?'

'You have to remember it's a bit different for me,' he said. 'In the past, because of the nature of my work, I've found myself in similar situations, whether in war zones or in the aftermath of some natural disaster, but actually…yes, this time I have to say it's been different for me, too.'

'In what way?' Once again Claire allowed her gaze to meet his, her pulse racing at the expression in his dark eyes.

'Well, firstly, I suppose,' he said, 'because my own personal safety was involved, and I think it's probably always difficult to get back to normal immediately after something like that…'

'And secondly?' she said, almost holding her breath as she waited for his answer.

'I think you already know the answer to that,' he replied softly.

In the silence that followed his words Claire felt something twist deep inside her, something she came to recognise as that same knot of desire she'd felt earlier when she'd allowed herself to fantasise and to ask the question, what if?

'I think,' he went on after a moment, the air between them almost crackling with tension, 'that we both know that in another time and another place things would have been very different between the two of us.'

'Dominic…' She half lifted one hand.

'It's all right,' he went on easily. 'I know the score. I know you are already committed elsewhere.'

'That's true,' she admitted, 'but I also know that in other circumstances…' She broke off, the words she'd left unsaid somehow more eloquent than those she had. 'But…' she took a deep breath '…I also know that, given the choice, I did not want to return to England right away as the others did.'

'You implied you needed more time to recuperate,' he

said with a slight shrug. 'Or maybe you wanted to make the most of the time you had left in Rome.'

'No,' she replied, 'it wasn't that. I wanted to spend more time with you.'

He stared at her for a long moment then, his gaze softening into tenderness, he said, 'In that case, I suggest we acknowledge what might have been between us and enjoy what time we have left together.'

'I think that sounds a wonderful idea,' she agreed.

'We have one full day left,' he went on. 'Let's try and relax, see a little more of this wonderful city and simply enjoy being together.' Leaning across the table, he refilled her glass.

'I'll drink to that,' she replied.

Afterwards Claire was to think of that last day in Rome that she and Dominic spent together as a moment of calm in a storm or an oasis in the heat of the desert but at the same time the precious memory of which would have to last her a lifetime. It was something which would have to be kept carefully filed in the recesses of her mind, to be taken out and relived at difficult or lonely moments in her life when Dominic seemed far away. Only by reliving those memories would she be reassured that they had actually happened.

After meeting for an early breakfast the following morning they decided to spend at least part of the day sightseeing and catching up on those things they had missed, the Colosseum being one of them where for a time they allowed themselves to be transported back to the time of its brutal and bloody past as they visualised the days of ancient Rome, the games watched by emperors and citizens alike and the fights between gladiators and wild animals.

'I'm glad I didn't live in those days,' said Claire with a sudden shiver in spite of the heat of the day. 'It's hard to believe that nowadays all that sort of thing is such an attraction for tourists...and even for children.'

'So will you not bring your children here when you return to Rome?' asked Dominic with a laugh as he took her arm and led her away.

'I doubt I'll have to make that sort of decision,' Claire replied lightly.

'Oh? And why's that?' For a moment Dominic looked puzzled.

'Mike doesn't want any more children,' she replied. She hadn't meant to mention Mike that day but something compelled her to explain. If she had hoped that Dominic might leave it there she was mistaken.

'But what about you?' he said, and momentarily he seemed appalled. 'What do you want? Surely you want children?'

'Well, yes.' Claire considered. 'I suppose I would have liked children of my own, but on the other hand I wouldn't want to force the issue with Mike over something so crucial—and, besides, we have Stephen and Emma.'

'Ah, yes,' said Dominic, 'Emma. A rather demanding young lady from what you've told me.'

'Not really.' Claire wrinkled her nose. 'She suffered badly when her parents split up and I think Mike does his best to make things up to her.'

'Shouldn't it be her mother doing that if she was the one responsible for breaking up the marriage?' asked Dominic wryly.

'Well, yes, I dare say,' Claire agreed, 'but I think she does so as well.'

'So will you and Mike be moving in together?' His voice was almost without expression as he asked the crucial question.

For the briefest of moments Claire considered saying no, that their relationship hadn't reached that stage and was never likely to, but that would have been a lie and she knew she could never lie to Dominic. Besides, hadn't she just implied that she and Mike had reached the stage of discussing whether or not they should have children? 'That's the plan, yes,' she admitted. 'Just as soon as he sells his house and finds somewhere else to live.'

They changed the subject after that to Claire's relief. She didn't want to talk about Mike and her life with him, not on this one special day she had allowed herself with Dominic.

Together they strolled through the ruins of ancient Rome, the morning sun warm on their shoulders, then sat at a table in a street café and enjoyed espresso coffee before entering the cool, magnificent splendour of the basilica of Santa Maria Maggiore, their footsteps matching the echo of countless pilgrims before them.

Once, during the course of that magical day while they were sitting in a leafy piazza on a low wall in the cooling spray from numerous fountains, Claire found herself studying Dominic's features as if by doing so she could imprint the memory of his face in her mind for ever.

And once again, as had happened before, as if he had the power to read her mind, he lifted his hand and with the tips of his fingers began to trace the line of her features as if he, too, was trying to record to memory the texture of her skin, the curve of her cheek or the gentle arch of an eyebrow. After a moment of almost unbearable sweetness Claire caught his hand and held it against her cheek then, when at last she looked up into his eyes, he bent his head and his lips briefly and gently touched hers. In that instant Rome seemed to come to a standstill. The roar of the traffic receded to a dull throb and as she closed her eyes in an attempt to capture the moment and install it in her memory the sun seemed to explode behind her eyelids in a golden blaze.

At the end of the day they opted not to dine at the hotel but to eat at an intimate little restaurant they had discovered in the course of their sightseeing. For that last night together Claire wore a dress of black with diamanté shoulder straps and matching jewelled sandals, which perfectly complemented her blonde hair and her golden skin kissed by the Italian sun.

Throughout the evening their mood changed from the fun and laughter they had shared throughout the day to one of quiet desperation as if each of them was only too aware that the hours were ticking away to that moment when they would have to part for ever. When they finally left the restaurant and strolled back through the narrow streets to the hotel it seemed the most natural thing in the world when Dominic slipped his arm around her. He felt familiar, safe and warm, just as he had that night when he had held her close while she had slept, but this time there was an added element to their closeness. This time desire was present and each of them knew that the other was only too aware of it.

On reaching the hotel, they took the stairs instead of the lift and by the time they reached Claire's room it was a foregone conclusion that Dominic would stay there and not continue on to his own room on the floor above.

'Are you sure?' he murmured as the door clicked shut behind them and he drew her into his arms. Hungrily, his gaze searching her eyes, he held her face, his thumbs beneath her jaw, fingers tangled in her hair.

'Oh, yes,' she whispered, and at last his lips met hers in a kiss, in itself full of fire and passion but which proved to be only a foretaste of what was to come.

When the black dress, chosen with such care, slid to the polished wooden floor, falling around her ankles in a dark pool, Claire raised her arms, sliding them around Dominic's neck and arching her body in a gesture of utter submission. Effortlessly he lifted her, swinging her up into his arms before carrying her to the large double bed with its covers of crisp white embroidered cotton.

She watched, loving every line of his firm, lean body as he undressed then, with his clothes discarded, he turned to face her and she gave a little sigh as he joined her, stretching out beside her on the bed before gathering her into his arms.

'There can be no more than this,' she told him later as once again he reached out for her, this time in the dead of night.

'I know that,' he replied, his sigh barely audible before he began caressing her and once more they visited that place whose piercing sweetness on their first visit had shaken Claire to the very core of her being.

She had stifled any feelings of guilt, knowing there would be time enough later for regret and recriminations—this one stolen night of love was for her and Dominic alone, a taste of what might have been to sustain them in the years to come, for already she knew that what she had found with this man would be like the man himself, utterly unforgettable.

CHAPTER SEVEN

IF CLAIRE had imagined that time spent with Dominic would in some way assuage her feelings and satisfy her longing she was mistaken, for that precious time spent together had the opposite effect and when it was over her craving to be with him was stronger than ever. In the end, because she could not bear the final moment of parting and of actually saying goodbye, she called a car and left for the airport a whole hour before she needed to when Dominic thought she was simply in her room, packing.

Her journey to the airport was like some exquisite form of torture for while the car carried her away from him she knew that while they were both in Rome at least they breathed the same air and that only a few miles separated them, but that once her flight took off every minute would put a greater distance between them. She saw him everywhere, of course. In a side street alongside the Vatican as they passed in the car—surely that was him, jacket slung over one shoulder, strolling over the sunlit cobbles? And later, at the airport, her heart leapt at the sight of a dark-haired man in a red shirt, until she realised he had a wife and three young children with him. Even the man in the seat in front of her on the aircraft looked vaguely familiar and had her staring at the way his hair curled slightly at the back of his neck, holding her breath, convinced that by some miracle of fate Dominic had got there before her and had booked on the same flight as herself, until, of course, he turned his head and she saw with disbelief that he was nothing like Dominic.

He filled her thoughts constantly—as she wondered how

he would react when he found she had gone without saying goodbye, whether he would be upset or relieved because he, too, hated farewells. And was he regretting even now what had happened between them? Somehow she doubted that for there had been genuine tenderness in the sex they had shared while for her the whole experience had been so wonderful that she doubted she would find such passion with anyone ever again.

Her head ached with tension and at last she leaned back and closed her eyes, shutting out the intense blue of the sky and the white banks of clouds, their edges dipped with gold from the early morning sun as the plane soared heavenwards, carrying her away from Dominic. In time the pain in her head subsided and she opened her eyes, but as she accepted a fruit juice from the air stewardess she doubted whether the pain in her heart would ever go.

Her first stab of guilt came when to her surprise she found Mike waiting for her at Gatwick. He was his usual, slightly dishevelled self, his expression harassed and his shirt crumpled as he scanned the disembarking passengers with narrowed eyes, and just for a moment her heart went out to him.

'This is a surprise,' she said as she hugged him. 'I thought you were on call.'

'I am really,' he said. 'I swapped with Susan.'

'So that you could come and meet me—that was kind.' Claire kissed his cheek.

'Well, there were a couple of things really,' he said as he took the trolley bearing her luggage from her. 'Emma wanted to go to a friend's house so I dropped her off first.'

'Oh,' she said, 'I see.' Suddenly she felt deflated, yet again second best to his daughter.

'So how are you?' Mike said a little later as she took her place beside him in the car. 'You've got a bit of colour, but not as much as I expected.'

'Well, no, it wasn't really that sort of holiday…'

'No, I suppose not. I guess sightseeing isn't quite the same as a beach holiday.' He paused. 'What about these earth tremors, then?' he asked. 'You say you went to Assisi?'

'Well, we set out for Assisi,' Claire replied, 'but the tremors prevented us from getting there.'

'Some of the mountain villages were badly affected,' said Mike. By this time they had left the airport and joined the traffic. 'There was quite a bit about it on the news,' he went on. 'I'm glad you didn't get caught up in it—could have been nasty, you know.'

'Yes, Mike.' She took a deep breath, about to tell him that actually she had been caught up in it and that, yes, it had been nasty, very nasty, but before she could do so he spoke again.

'Emma's exams went all right,' he said.

'Really?' she said faintly.

'Yes, I'm glad they are over. She was getting rather stressed about them. Oh, talking of stress, Ben Lewis has stopped work now.'

'I thought he wasn't starting his sabbatical until next month.' Claire cast Mike a sidelong glance and found herself unmoved by the sight of his profile. He had a nice profile and usually it evoked feelings of tenderness in her, but today she felt nothing. In fact, apart from that one stab of guilt or remorse or whatever it had been when she'd first caught sight of him at the airport, she'd felt strangely devoid of any kind of feeling.

'He wasn't.' Mike shook his head. 'But there was some incident with a patient during the week and he got so stressed out that Richard signed him off.'

'Do we have a replacement for him?'

'No, not yet.' Mike shook his head again. 'It's a bit chaotic, to say the least.' He carried on talking about practice matters, and although Claire had been gearing herself up to tell him about all that had happened, she found herself abandoning the idea as a wave of fatigue suddenly hit her. There would be time enough later for all that, she told herself. She was suddenly missing Dominic terribly, as if by listening to Mike and easing back into her old life Dominic was slipping away from her. She didn't want that to happen and certainly not yet. She wanted to be alone, to think about all that had happened and then to relive every detail of those precious hours they had shared.

With a little sigh she turned her head and looked out of the window at the relentless British rain drenching everything in sight and the clouds of spray thrown up from the wheels of other vehicles on the motorway ahead. Italy suddenly seemed a world away—the warm sunshine, the blue skies, the laughter of the friends they had made, even the fear and the drama, and Dominic. Of course, Dominic. For it was because of Dominic that Claire knew her life would never be quite the same again.

Mike took her straight home to the Edwardian, red-bricked house in the heart of the Surrey town of Hazelwood where for the past few years Claire had rented the top-floor flat. He carried her bags up the three flights of stairs for her, dumping them on the sitting-room floor as she picked up her mail.

'Will you stay, Mike,' she asked, 'for a cup of tea? I'll put the kettle on.'

'No,' he said, 'I can't stop, I have to go and pick Emma up now.' He gave her a hug, putting his arms around her and for a moment holding her close. Claire hated herself because she was relieved he wasn't able to stay. He felt warm and safe and familiar, but…he wasn't Dominic.

'Thanks for coming to meet me, Mike,' she said when he at last released her.

'No problem.' he smiled. 'It's good to have you home,

Claire. Shame I'm on call this weekend. We'll have to spend some time together later.'

'Yes, of course. I'll see you at work.'

After he had gone she stood for a moment looking round at her flat. It looked strange and a little dull in spite of the recently decorated walls and the rich blues of the rugs and cushions. The dullness must, she thought, be something to do with the vibrant, sun-kissed colours of Italy that she still carried in her head. It was silent, too, overwhelmingly silent, and every moment she expected, even willed the phone to ring, for it to be Dominic, which was crazy, impossible even, for hadn't it been she who had said there was to be nothing more between them, she who had insisted that they shouldn't even exchange addresses or phone numbers? For she had known with intuitive certainty that any further contact between them would be her undoing.

Had that been ridiculous? she asked herself now as misery threatened to overwhelm her. Would it really have mattered if they had decided to keep in touch? Deep down she knew it would, for she knew that it wouldn't have ended there. Sooner or later a meeting would have been arranged and it would have been almost inevitable for them to pick up where they had left off. Wonderful as that may have been, it would have led to her being forced to make a choice between Mike and Dominic—she couldn't have both.

And on the other hand, she told herself firmly, in allowing her mind to race ahead wasn't she in danger of assuming too much? There was simply no knowing whether Dominic would want that sort of relationship anyway, even if she was free. By his own admission he found commitment difficult, preferring to be something of a free spirit himself and be able to take off for the world's trouble spots as and when he chose to do so. It was one thing to have a brief fling with a woman he'd met on holiday, a woman whom he knew he had little chance of ever seeing again. It was something else entirely to start a long-term affair that would inevitable carry a deep commitment to each other.

And wasn't that also what she had wanted? she asked herself ruthlessly as a little later she unpacked her bags and loaded the washing machine with her holiday clothes. Hadn't she gone utterly and completely against character and allowed herself a wild, passionate encounter with a virtual stranger safe in the sure knowledge that she would be highly unlikely to set eyes on him ever again? Of course she had, she told herself firmly.

So, if that was the case, why was she now still feeling so desperately miserable? She should have been able to file Dominic under delightful memories, a bit like holiday photographs, to be taken out and pored over on dark winter days. She should have been looking forward to seeing Mike, to settling once again into the comfortable ritual that their relationship had become. She should have been able to simply slip back into the routine of her life with maybe just the smallest of sighs of regret, but she was unable to do any of those things because her head was full of the warmth and splendour of Italy and her heart and senses were full of a man called Dominic.

'Good holiday, Claire?'

It was two days later and Claire had returned to her job at the Hargreaves Centre. Her friend and fellow practice nurse, Penny Riley, had just joined her in one of the treatment rooms.

'Er, yes, pretty good, thanks,' Claire replied.

'You don't sound too sure,' said Penny, peering closely at her. 'Mind you, it couldn't have been too much fun, having to go on your own like that at the last minute. Bit dull, was it?'

'Actually, no, it was anything but dull,' Claire replied with a wry smile.

'Really?' Penny raised her eyebrows. 'Tell me more. Sounds interesting.'

'Well, I got a bit caught up in the earth tremors.'

'Did you?' Penny stared at her. 'We wondered about that at the time, but we came to the conclusion you were miles away from any of that.'

'Well, I was, or rather I would have been if I'd stayed in Rome,' said Claire. 'Trouble was, I took a trip to Assisi on the day in question.'

'Assisi?' Penny had started to check some supplies that had just been delivered but she looked up sharply. 'Heavens, wasn't that near the affected area?'

'Yes.' Claire nodded. She'd not spoken of it until now. Mike hadn't pursued the matter further and she'd found it easier not to bring it up again, even avoiding the issue with anyone else. But somehow Penny was different—Penny was her friend and they shared most things. 'In actual fact I was in a building that partially collapsed,' she admitted.

'Good grief!' Penny stared at her. 'What happened?'

'We'd gone into this building—it was an old monastery that is used as a museum these days...'

'Who's "we"?' interrupted Penny curiously.

'The people I was travelling with.' Claire swallowed. 'It was a coach party with people from the hotel I was staying in and some people from other hotels in Rome,' she added. She suddenly had a mental picture of them all taking their seats on the coach on that fateful morning.

'I see, yes, go on,' Penny urged.

'Well, we'd stopped off at this monastery,' Claire continued. 'It was high up in the hills just outside Assisi. We'd had a look at the church and the cloisters and we were in this huge room that had once been the monks' refectory when there were these terrible rumbling and cracking noises.'

'Was there no other warning?' asked Penny.

'Not really.' Claire wrinkled her nose. 'Although there was a strange sort of atmosphere that day—sort of electric, like waiting for something to happen. A bit like before a thunderstorm,' she added, remembering Dominic's predictions. As the memory of him sitting at the table in the street café on that first day they had spoken came into her mind, a sudden pain stabbed at her heart and she gulped. 'Anyway,' she went on at last, wondering whether Penny could possibly tell just how bad she was feeling, 'like I say, the building we were in partially collapsed. The tremors must have caused a rift to open up underneath it, splitting some of the outer walls and dislodging the foundations. A huge section of the roof caved in, showering us with debris, and pillars and statues came crashing down all around us...'

Penny stared at her, aghast. 'It must have been terrifying!' she exclaimed.

'It was.' Claire nodded and as once again she heard those noises in her head and in her mouth tasted the choking dust she found that her hands were shaking.

'Was anyone injured?' asked Penny.

'Oh, yes,' Claire replied quietly. 'Several people were injured, some quite badly.'

'You could have all been killed!'

'I know.' Claire paused, unable for a moment to carry on, seeing only too clearly in her mind's eye what at the time had appeared to be that bundle of dusty rags. 'In fact,' she went on at last, 'someone was killed.'

'How dreadful!' Penny stared at her, obviously shocked and horrified at what she was hearing. 'Was it someone you knew?'

'No.' Claire shook her head. 'It was an elderly man whom we believe was working at the monastery. It was terrible really…poor man. Some of the party from my hotel were injured,' she went on after a moment. 'One woman had severe head injuries—she went into a coma and I later heard she had developed a blood clot. A man suffered a crushed femur, another lady had a heart attack and arrested. Oh, and just for good measure, another young woman was twelve weeks pregnant and thought she was about to miscarry…' She paused. 'And quite apart from all that, practically everyone suffered cuts and bruises.'

'They must have been glad to have you there,' said Penny in awe.

'Well, yes, I guess so,' Claire agreed. Taking a deep breath, she added, 'Actually, there was a doctor in the party as well.'

'That was a stroke of luck.' Penny looked surprised. 'It isn't often that happens. Doctors are a bit like policemen in my experience, never around when you want one.'

'I know.' Claire nodded. 'The trouble was, we had very few resources—it was improvisation all the way.'

'What did you do?' Penny was obviously intrigued now.

'Ripped up garments for bandages and pressure pads, used table legs for splints. I tell you, I'd never been so pleased in my life to find I had a packet of wet wipes in my bag.'

'What about the woman who arrested?' asked Penny curiously.

'We did basic resuscitation.'

'You and the doctor?'

'Yes.' Claire gulped. 'Me and the doctor.'

'And did she survive?'

'Oh, yes. The last I heard she was about to be discharged from an Assisi hospital in order to fly back to the UK.'

'It sounds as if you coped admirably,' said Penny.

'Well, we did our best,' Claire replied with a little shrug.

'The worst bit, apart from lack of medical resources, was the fact that we had very little to eat or drink.'

'So how long were you in there, for heaven's sake?' Penny's large blue eyes widened.

'Um...about thirty hours altogether, I think...'

'Thirty hours!' Penny almost choked. 'You mean you were there overnight?'

'Oh, yes,' Claire replied. 'You see, we weren't the only ones needing to be rescued. Several of the villages round about had been badly hit. People had been killed or badly injured, houses had been demolished...the rescue services were stretched to their limits...' She broke off, unable to continue as in a sudden, rather terrifying flashback, memories came flooding back. For a moment she was right there again amidst the chaos—the moans and screams, the battles to stop the bleeding on Diane's and Peter's head wounds, the crude efforts to set Ted's leg and try to alleviate his pain and then the desperate attempt to resuscitate Evelyn.

'It sounds absolutely dreadful,' said Penny in consternation. Peering at Claire again, she said, 'Claire, you're shaking...'

'No, I'm all right,' Claire protested. 'Really I am...'

'But you've been through a dreadful experience.'

'I was one of the lucky ones—I wasn't even injured.' She didn't say why she had escaped injury, that it had been because Dominic had shielded her body. There was no way she could put that into words, not even to Penny.

'Even so...' Penny shook her head '...psychologically it must have been devastating.' She paused. 'Didn't you have *any* water or food?'

'We had one bottle of mineral water,' Claire replied, 'one can of Coke and one of some fizzy orange drink. Some people had sweets—peppermints and barley sugar, that sort of thing.'

'And that was it?' asked Penny incredulously. 'How many of you were there, for heaven's sake?'

'Eighteen of us all together,' Claire answered, then as an afterthought added, 'It got a bit difficult at times, I can tell you, what with having to set up a latrine in one corner of the room and having a dead body in the other.'

'Oh, good grief.' Penny's hand flew to her mouth as if that aspect of the ordeal hadn't occurred to her before. 'And then, I suppose,' she went on after a moment, 'you had the heat to contend with as well?'

'Well, it was hot outside certainly,' Claire agreed, 'but actually in the monastery itself it was cool and during the night it got really cold. The trouble was, most of us were only wearing thin summer clothes. One of the ladies had a cardigan and someone had a sweater which we used as best we could to cover up the injured.'

'So how did you keep warm?' asked Penny. She was clearly appalled at what she was hearing.

'We had to huddle together,' said Claire.

They were silent for a moment. 'What about the doctor?' asked Penny suddenly.

'What about him?' Claire looked up sharply, afraid that Penny, who knew her so well, was even now reading her mind, that in some way she knew what had happened, that it had been Dominic who had held her through that night to keep her warm, and at the same time she would know how much she was missing him.

'Well, was he injured?'

'Oh, yes,' she replied, relieved that was all Penny had meant. 'A piece of masonry fell on his shoulder. I…I managed to dress it for him as best I could.'

'So was he elderly, this doctor?'

'No, he wasn't elderly—quite young really…' Suddenly she found she couldn't bear to even talk about him. 'Penny,' she said in sudden desperation, anything to change the subject, to steer the conversation away from what had happened next, afraid in some way that Penny would detect something amiss, 'I really must get on.' She glanced at her watch. 'I have a clinic starting in five minutes and I haven't prepared anything.'

'I'm not even sure that you should be here,' said Penny doubtfully.

'What do you mean?' Claire stared at her friend.

'You've had a severe shock, you've been through a terrible experience and I think you need some time to recuperate.'

'Nonsense.' Mentally Claire pulled herself together, trying to banish all thoughts of Dominic, at least until after she'd taken the morning clinic. 'I'm perfectly all right. Like I told you, I was one of the lucky ones. There were others far worse off than me.'

'Even so...' Penny sounded far from convinced but, not giving her time to protest further, Claire collected the supplies and notes she needed and made her way to her own treatment room.

It turned out to be a fairly average Monday morning and Claire's clinic was like countless others she had taken, with injections to be given, blood to be taken for testing, dressings on leg ulcers to be changed and plaster checks to be carried out on broken limbs.

Some of her patients were delighted to see her back and wanted to know about her holiday. She, however, was evasive when they asked about Italy and the fact that it had been in the news.

'We were worried about you,' said one elderly lady as Claire changed the dressings on her ankle. 'I said to my Cyril, that's where my nurse has gone and that I hoped you would be all right. Then someone here said you'd gone to Rome and Rome hadn't been hit so we thought you probably were all right.'

She didn't enlighten the patient or any of the others who asked, concentrating instead on how wonderful Rome had been, how warm the weather and how friendly the Italians. By the end of her clinic she was exhausted, and when Mike strode in as the last patient left she was practically incapable of offering any resistance.

'Why didn't you tell me?' he demanded.

'Tell you what?' she said warily.

'About what happened to you in Italy?'

'I—' She was about to say that he hadn't asked but he gave her no time.

'I've been talking to Penny,' he said.

'She shouldn't have said anything,' protested Claire with a weak, dismissive little gesture.

'I'm glad she did,' said Mike. 'She was worried about you, Claire.'

'I'm all right, Mike, really I am.'

'It sounds as if you were right in the thick of things. Penny said a building collapsed around you, is that right?'

'Well, yes...'

'That someone was killed, others were badly injured...'

'Yes, but—'

'That you were trapped for over twenty-four hours with precious little water or food?'

'Yes, but, Mike, listen, please. I wasn't injured,' she protested. 'I was one of the lucky ones.'

'There is such a thing as post-traumatic stress syndrome,' said Mike. 'You of all people should know that.'

'Well, yes, of course I know, but I can assure you I'm not suffering from that.'

'You mean because you are a nurse you are immune to that sort of thing? Like Ben couldn't accept the fact that he was stressed out, that it couldn't happen to him because he is a doctor?'

'Mike, please, I know what you're saying.' Claire lifted her hands in protest. 'You're wrong. I'm fine, really I am.'

'Penny said you were very shaky earlier on,' Mike persisted.

'Maybe I was, just for a while when I was telling her about it,' Claire admitted, 'but I'm OK now. I just want to forget about it and put it behind me.'

'Sorry, Claire.' Mike stepped forward and, taking her chin tilted her face so that she was forced to look up into his. 'I'm going to pull rank here. I want you to have some counselling and after that you are to take at least another week off. So, no arguments, because that's the way it's going to be.'

CHAPTER EIGHT

CLAIRE went to visit her father in Portsmouth. A visit was long overdue and in the end it seemed the perfect arrangement—the combination of a period of enforced recuperation following a couple of counselling sessions and the opportunity to spend some uninterrupted family time.

In recent years, following the death of his wife and his own retirement from his job with the Ministry of Defence, Claire's father, Tom, had lived with his unmarried sister Marjorie in a bungalow on the outskirts of the naval town, which had been home since Claire's childhood. They were both delighted to see Claire and when she was forced to give a reason for her impromptu visit they set about spoiling her and making her stay as pleasant as they could.

Once she had recounted the story of what had happened in Italy little more was said about it and her days were spent lazing in the garden, on trips out to lunch or on long walks on the beach with her father's dog, Bosun.

Gradually the images of what had happened in Italy, which had been razor sharp in her mind, began to blur slightly at the edges and even the intense, heightened emotion she had felt for Dominic began to recede and take its place in her memory. She began to recognise that what she had felt for him had most probably been a reaction to circumstances.

In the first place, the initial attraction between them had been fuelled by the magic of Italy itself and the exhilaration of a holiday situation. What had followed had changed everything and determined the course of events—the drama, the heightened tension of the life-and-death situation and the fact that she and Dominic had been thrown so closely together in taking leading roles in caring for their companions.

As all this became clear Claire felt herself begin to relax and to let go. She would never see Dominic again. She knew that, just as she knew that eventually she would have to put all thoughts of what had happened between them right out of her mind and get on with the rest of her life.

It wasn't going to be easy. She faced that fact on one of her early morning walks with Bosun across an endless expanse of hard wet sand as black-headed gulls wheeled and dipped above her, their plaintive cries mingling with the sounds of shipping in the Solent. Dominic had had a profound effect on her and what they had shared had shaken her to the very depths of her being, not least because she'd never experienced it before, not with Mike or with anyone else. But the fact that it was over eventually helped her to concentrate her mind. Mike loved her, she was pretty sure of that. He sometimes had rather a detached way of showing it but deep down she knew he cared for her. No one knew what had taken place between herself and Dominic and Mike wasn't likely to ever hear about it. She had to forget him, she told herself firmly for the umpteenth time, forget him and get on with her life.

'So what's happening with you and Mike?' asked her father one morning as they sat together in the garden of the bungalow. Marjorie had gone shopping and they were alone, the only sounds those of a neighbour as he mowed his grass and an occasional whimper from Bosun as he twitched and chased rabbits in his dreams.

'What do you mean?' Claire cast Tom a glance and momentarily felt a pang as it suddenly hit her that he was looking older.

'Well, is marriage on the cards?' he asked.

'I don't know about that.' Claire shook her head. 'We

may live together.' She paused. 'Would that bother you?' she asked.

'Probably not if you were happy with it,' he replied.

'But you would rather I was married.' It was hardly a question.

Her father leaned back in his chair. 'I'm a bit old-fashioned, Claire,' he said with his slow smile, 'but, yes, if I'm honest, I would like to see you happily married.'

'It doesn't bother you that Mike's been married before—that he already has a family?' asked Claire tentatively.

'I don't think so.' Tom slowly shook his head. 'I like Mike, and again if it's what you want... I must admit, though, I had always imagined—your mother and I had always imagined,' he corrected himself, 'you getting married and having children of your own. Will Mike want more children?' he added uncertainly.

'No, Dad, I don't think so.'

'That's a pity,' said Tom, rubbing his chin. 'It would have been nice for you to have children of your own.'

Her father's words had echoed what Dominic had said and she felt a sudden pang deep inside, but what Dominic had said mustn't matter now, she told herself fiercely, she had to put him right out of her mind.

'You do love him, don't you?' Her father broke into her thoughts.

'Who, Mike?' she said. For one wild moment, because she had been thinking about him, she thought her father had meant Dominic.

'Of course Mike,' said Tom mildly, adding with a touch of curiosity, 'Who did you think I meant?'

'Oh, nothing,' she said quickly. 'No one. Of course I love Mike. He's a dear man and the children, Emma and Stephen—they're great.'

She didn't mention Mike's ex-wife Jan and how difficult she could be, especially over the children's visits, and finances…always finances, in spite of the fact that Mike had been incredibly generous after the divorce. She didn't mention how the children, Emma especially, viewed her with suspicion, casting her as some sort of witch or ogre who had been responsible for luring her father away when nothing could have been further from the truth. And neither did she mention that, having believed herself to be in love with Mike, she had found herself doubting it when she had found such fulfilment in the arms of another man. How could she? How could she say any of those things, especially to her father who loved her and only had her welfare and happiness at heart?

'Don't worry about me,' she heard herself say. 'I'm absolutely fine and when I get back to work and settled down again you and Auntie Marjorie must come up and stay for a weekend, then you can meet the children.'

In a way Claire was pleased to be going back to work. She had sorted things out in her mind now and she needed to throw herself into her work in an effort to finally put her memories to rest.

It was a warm, pleasant summer's day—she was to remember that afterwards—and she walked from her flat to the Hargreaves Centre rather than take her car. She met Richard Hargreaves, the senior partner, on the steps outside the building and he seemed genuinely pleased to see her.

'Claire,' he said, pausing for a moment, 'nice to see you back. Is all well?'

'Yes, thank you, Richard,' she replied, 'and it's nice to be back.'

They entered the building together and were forced to push their way through the hordes of patients waiting in Reception, some wanting appointments, others leaving or collecting repeat prescriptions, others requesting home visits, and to Claire it was just like countless other mornings.

Phones were ringing and being answered by the receptionists, only to ring again immediately as the calls were completed. Together with Richard, she made her way down the corridor, past the consulting and treatment rooms to the staffroom.

The room was crowded and as they entered Claire caught a glimpse of Mike who was talking to Susan Bridges, another of the practice partners. Penny was there in conversation with Christopher Abbott, the junior partner, and others; ancillary staff and members of the community team were checking on their work schedules for the day.

'Claire!' Mike caught sight of her, left Susan's side and made his way across the room to her side. 'Everything all right?' he asked. He'd phoned her the previous evening when she had arrived back from Portsmouth but they had not yet seen each other.

'Hello, Mike.' She smiled. 'Yes, everything's fine.'

It was good to be back, she realised, looking around, to be surrounded by her colleagues and her friends and Mike, of course. She was lucky, she knew that.

'Claire...' Mike had turned away to speak to someone but he turned back now and took her arm. 'You haven't met Ben's replacement, have you? We've been incredibly lucky to get a locum so quickly.' As he was speaking he moved and a man who had been standing slightly behind him talking to Bridget, another of the partners, turned towards her.

Claire had heard people say that in certain situations their hearts had stood still, and she hadn't really believed them, had imagined it impossible for one's heart to stop, but at that moment she was convinced that was exactly what happened. In that one frozen moment it was as if the world tilted slightly on its axis, as if the chatter of her colleagues seemed to recede, as if the edges of her vision blurred and condensed as she found herself gazing at Dominic.

The sight of him was so dear and so very familiar, from the clean-cut lines of his features to his dark eyes and the set of his head, that for the briefest of moments she never even questioned why he was there. She only knew as her heart suffused with sudden, indescribable joy that he was.

Vaguely, as if from a great distance, she was aware that Mike was making introductions.

'Claire, this is Dominic Hansford. Dominic, Claire Schofield. Claire is one of our practice nurses,' he explained. 'In actual fact she will be working with you—taking your clinics as she is the nurse assigned to Ben and to Susan. Claire also takes sessions in our stress-counselling programme.'

'Is that right? How interesting.' Dominic inclined his head slightly and if Mike noticed that Claire didn't extend her hand he didn't comment on the fact.

'Dominic has been working abroad with children's charities,' Mike went on enthusiastically.

'Really?' Claire's voice sounded to her as if it came from a long way off. 'So whatever brings him to the Hargreaves Centre?' she finally managed to add.

'I am between assignments,' Dominic replied coolly. 'I have recently been working in A and E in a hospital in Warwickshire and my boss there is a friend of Richard Hargreaves.'

'Fortunately for us,' said Mike with a laugh. 'We were getting worried, I can tell you. What with Ben having to go off early, there was no time to advertise and carry out the usual interviews. To have someone who comes so highly recommended is an absolute godsend—isn't that right, Claire?'

'Yes.' Somehow she answered, although she was still feeling that she might be in danger of fainting.

'I'm afraid we're rather chucking you in at the deep end,

old man,' said Mike ruefully, turning to Dominic, 'but Claire will soon show you the ropes, won't you, Claire?'

She didn't answer, she couldn't, because she was still in shock and it was only gradually that the questions began to teem into her brain. What was Dominic doing here? Why had he come back into her life when they had agreed that what had happened between them was at an end?

Just for a moment, after the shock at seeing him, when her heart had started beating again, her pulse had begun racing as it sank in that he was actually there beside her, that if she reached out her hand she could touch him.

But then, in no time at all, the impossibility of the situation hit her. She hadn't been able to bring herself to meet his gaze again and with a murmured excuse slipped away to the changing room. As she changed into the smart, navy-blue sister's uniform she wore for work she found she was shaking and was forced to get a firm grip on herself. Here she was having spent the last week recovering from all that had happened in Italy, returning to work ready to pick up the pieces of her life again, only to have Dominic stroll back and turn her world upside down.

She couldn't for one moment imagine what he was thinking of in coming there. He had told her that he was returning abroad and that he had finished at his present job, but before that he was supposed to have been travelling on to Prague after leaving Italy. That, of course, had been his plan before that last fateful night in Rome, which they had spent together, but surely it couldn't be because of that that he had changed his plans? Claire was sure she had made it perfectly plain that there could be nothing else between them, that she was committed to Mike and that shortly she and Mike would be moving in together. So what was he doing here? she asked herself in desperation. The last thing she wanted was for Mike to find out what had happened in Italy. Come to that, she wouldn't be too keen on any of the others knowing either. It was pretty obvious that Dominic had not yet told anyone at the centre that they had met before, because if he had Mike would have been certain to have said something, instead of simply introducing them in the way he had, so the thing to do was to make sure it stayed that way. Before that, however, she needed to know why he was there.

Smoothing down her uniform, Claire strode out of the changing room and down the corridor to Ben Lewis's consulting room. She had to sort this out now, once and for all. There was no way she could take a clinic or concentrate on work of any description until she had had this matter out with Dominic.

She barely knocked on the door, just a perfunctory tap, pushing the door open as he replied, bidding her enter. She had been geared up to tackle him, fired up to demand an explanation, but as he looked up at her from behind the desk where he was seated and her eyes met his all such notions flew out of the window and she found herself helplessly gazing at him, transported in that instant back to Rome and that delicious, forbidden interlude they had shared.

'Hi,' he said softly at last.

'Dominic…' Her voice was husky.

'I was expecting you. Come in.' He indicated for her to close the door. 'Sit down.'

Taking a deep breath in order to steady her nerves, Claire shut the door but ignored his offer of a chair, preferring instead to stand as if looking down at him would gain her some advantage.

'What are you doing here?' she managed to say at last, and surprised even herself at how firm her voice sounded. She had been afraid it would come out as a demented squawk.

'I would have thought that was obvious,' Dominic replied calmly. 'I've taken the job of locum to replace Ben—'

'Yes, I know that,' Claire interrupted him impatiently. 'What I want to know is why. How did you know about the job?' she demanded.

'You told me about it,' he replied mildly.

She stared at him. 'I didn't—' she began, only to have him interrupt her.

'Yes, you did. That first time that we met by the Trevi fountain—we went for that drink and you told me all about the Hargreaves Centre and that one of the partners had become so stressed out that he needed to take a sabbatical. You also said the centre would be looking for a locum to replace him.'

Claire frowned. 'Well, yes, maybe I did, but I didn't for one moment imagine you might be interested in such a job.'

'Why not?' There was a hint of amusement now in those brown eyes.

'Well, you seemed perfectly happy with what you were doing—with your work abroad and even with the temporary hospital work you were doing.'

'So are you saying that if you'd known I might have been interested, you wouldn't have said anything?' Dominic raised his eyebrows questioningly.

'No…well, I might have done, but that was then, before…'

'Before what, Claire?' he said softly.

'You know what before,' she retorted. 'What happened afterwards changed everything.'

'It certainly did,' he replied.

'So why have you done it? Why are you here?' There was an edge of something almost bordering on hysteria in her voice.

'Because I had to.' The amusement was gone now and the tenderness in his voice threw her a little.

'But why…?' she whispered. 'Why…?'

'You know why. I couldn't just leave things the way they were.'

'But we agreed,' she protested, 'you know we did. I told you there could never be anything between us.'

'I know, but there *is* something between us—you know it as well as I do.'

'Yes…but…'

'You went,' he said, and there was mild reproach in his voice now. 'You went without saying goodbye.'

'I'm sorry,' she whispered. 'I had to, I couldn't bear… it…'

'So you do feel something for me?'

'Of course I do, Dominic,' she cried, 'you know I do!' Distractedly she ran her fingers through her hair. 'But it doesn't alter anything. I still have Mike…'

'Ah, yes, Mike,' said Dominic.

'What do you mean?' Claire stared at him. 'Why do you say it like that? What's wrong with Mike?' she demanded.

'Nothing,' he said innocently, shaking his head, 'there's nothing at all wrong with Mike. He seems a decent sort of guy…but…'

'But what?' said Claire suspiciously.

'Nothing.' He shook his head.

'No, go on,' she persisted. 'I want to know. What did you mean?'

'Just that he wasn't what I had expected, that's all.'

'In what way?' She was on the defensive now.

'I don't know. Nothing really. I suppose I expected him to be younger, that's all.' He shrugged.

'He's not old,' Claire protested. 'He's only forty-two, for heaven's sake.'

'Really?' Dominic raised his eyebrows. 'I would have thought he was older—maybe it's because he looks harassed most of the time.'

'He has a great deal on his plate,' said Claire firmly. 'There's tremendous pressure here in the practice, especially since Ben went, and then there are his children for whom he feels very responsible…'

'And his ex-wife,' said Dominic, nodding.

'His ex-wife?' Claire frowned. 'What's she got to do with anything?'

'She was here when I came in last week to meet everyone. She seems a very…determined sort of lady.'

'Yes, she is,' Claire was forced to reply. She was silent for a moment. 'How did you get to be here so soon?' she asked curiously. 'What about references and things?'

'No need for anything like that,' said Dominic with a shrug. 'Like Mike said, my boss, Alistair Raeburn, at the hospital where I had been working happens to be a golfing friend of Richard Hargreaves—when you said you worked here it rang a bell and then I remembered I'd heard Alistair talk of Richard. I contacted Alistair, told him I was applying for the locum post here, and when I asked him if I could use his name he agreed. In the end I think Richard Hargreaves was so relieved to get someone it wouldn't have really mattered who it was—the fact that I had worked for a friend of his was a bonus.'

'But I thought you were going abroad again,' Claire protested.

'I probably will eventually,' Dominic replied evenly, 'but my dad isn't fully recovered yet, my contract at the hospital is finished and quite apart from all that I wanted to see you again.'

'What happened to Prague…to Austria?' she asked in ever-growing desperation.

'They can wait,' he replied. 'I'm sure they will still be there when I get around to visiting them.'

She gazed at him helplessly again for a long moment.

'No one here knows,' she said at last, 'about us, about me meeting you in Italy...'

'I didn't for one moment imagine anyone did,' he said quietly. 'So what did you tell them?' he asked after a moment.

'Well, they know all about the earthquake, of course—they also know that I was trapped with others in the monastery, they know that some of the others were badly injured...and...and that there was a doctor in the party...' She trailed off, uncertain how to continue.

'But presumably they didn't know my name?'

'No,' she shook her head.

'I didn't think they did,' he said. 'It certainly didn't seem to ring any bells when I was introduced to everyone.'

'Have you told anyone you have just returned from Italy?' asked Claire sharply.

'No.' He shook his head. 'As soon as I realised that you hadn't mentioned my name to anyone I decided it best if I kept quiet.'

'Well, I suppose that's something,' said Claire with a sudden sense of relief. 'I want it to stay that way, Dominic,' she added.

'As you wish.' He shrugged.

'It has to,' said Claire in sudden desperation. 'It can't come out now that we know each other, that we were together in Italy, otherwise everyone will wonder why I didn't say more about you when I got back and why you didn't say anything when you first got here.'

'OK.' He nodded. 'We'll keep quiet about it. As far as anyone else here is concerned, we have only just set eyes on each other and it'll stay that way for as long as I remain here.'

'You intend staying?' asked Claire in dismay. Somehow she had imagined he would say that now he would move on.

'Of course. I've already signed a six-month contract.'

She stared at him. 'Six months!'

'Yes,' he said. Looking up at her, he added, 'is that going to be a problem for you, Claire?'

She took a deep breath. 'Of course not,' she said firmly at last, 'just as long as you fully understand the situation.'

'And what situation is that?' he asked softly, that hint of amusement back in his voice now.

'That Mike and I are an item and that what happened between you and me has to be forgotten.'

'We'll see,' he said in the same soft tone then, more briskly and rising to his feet, he added, 'I guess we'd better get down to some work. I understand this is to be my consulting room and that you are to be my practice nurse so maybe we could start by you showing me where everything is.'

It turned out to be one of the most difficult days of Claire's life. Even showing Dominic the ropes and where everything was in the surgery was far from easy because with every step she took, every movement she made, she was only too aware of the presence of the man at her side, of all they had shared and of what, briefly, they had meant to each other.

The others, mercifully, and Mike especially seemed totally unaware of any undercurrents between herself and the new locum and the only reference to him came while he was still in morning surgery and Claire briefly met up with Penny in the practice storeroom.

'I say,' said Penny, glancing over her shoulder to make sure she wasn't being overheard, 'he's rather gorgeous, isn't he?'

'Who?' said Claire, deciding on the spur of the moment to play dumb.

'Well, him, the new locum. Dominic or whatever he calls himself.'

'Oh, him,' said Claire vaguely.

'Don't you think so?' said Penny in surprise.

'Don't I think what?' Claire frowned.

'Well, that he's gorgeous, of course.'

'Er, yes, I suppose so.' Claire shrugged. 'If you like that sort of thing.'

'Oh, yes,' said Penny with a laugh. 'I do...' She paused. 'Don't you?' She added curiously.

'Yes, I guess so,' Claire replied in the same noncommittal tone, 'but you forget, I'm spoken for. It wouldn't do for me to go round singing the praises of a newcomer, would it?'

'No, I guess not.' Penny paused. 'Nor me, I suppose,' she added ruefully. 'But if I was single again...and a few years younger, I can tell you...Dr Dominic Hansford would have to watch out.' She laughed. 'I tell you something else, though,' she said, 'he's caused no end of a stir amongst the receptionists.'

'Has he?' said Claire weakly.

'Well, you can imagine, can't you?' Penny laughed. 'The minute they set eyes on him when he came in last week they were falling over themselves trying to attract his attention, and from what I can make out this morning they've got bets going as to which one of them he will ask out first.'

'Oh,' said Claire, 'really?' She paused then, taking a deep breath, she said, 'Do they know that he is free?'

'Well, we know he isn't married,' said Penny. 'Susan told us that—he was asked that when he signed his contract and I guess as far as the girls are concerned that's all that matters. All I can say is, Dominic Hansford, watch out.'

Claire turned away, suddenly sick at heart as she began taking dressing packs out of the cupboard. During the morning she had almost come to terms with the fact that she was going to have to work alongside Dominic for the next six months, and that was bad enough, but the prospect of him being involved with another member of staff whilst he was there was something else entirely and not something she even wanted to contemplate.

CHAPTER NINE

'I WOULD like the doctor to take a look at your leg today, Mrs Hendy, before we put another dressing on,' said Claire, speaking loudly for the benefit of her elderly patient who was rather hard of hearing.

The old lady looked up in alarm. 'Why?' she demanded. 'There's nothing wrong with it, is there?'

'No.' Claire shook her head then, hastening to reassure her, she added, 'The ulcer is healing nicely but there's a bit of swelling around it so we'll just let Doctor have a look at it.'

'It isn't Dr Lewis, is it?' Mrs Hendy sounded suspicious now.

'No, it isn't,' Claire replied. 'It's Dr Hansford.'

'Never heard of him,' said the old lady with a loud sniff.

'That's because he's new,' said Claire with a smile. 'He's taken Dr Lewis's place for a while.'

'What's he like?' Mrs Hendy still sounded dubious.

'Well, he's a very good doctor,' replied Claire guardedly. Dominic had been at the Hargreaves Centre for several days now but she still found it incredibly difficult talking about him to anyone.

'I didn't mean that. What I meant was what's he like as a person?'

Claire took a deep breath. 'He's nice,' she said at last. 'You'll like him.'

Mrs Hendy peered up at Claire from beneath the brim of the straw sunhat she was wearing. 'Do you like him?' she said.

'Oh, yes.' Claire swallowed. 'Like I say—he's nice.' Her

tone, she hoped, was casual but inside, silently, she was screaming. Like him? I adore him!

As if to compound her feelings and to frustrate her even further, Dominic, at that moment, right on cue, came into the treatment room. If she had thought he'd looked handsome in Italy in casual holiday clothes her heart turned over now as he strolled into the room in a crisp white shirt and a pair of beautifully tailored trousers, his hair tamed with gel so that it looked even darker than usual. Immediately his eyes met hers. 'Sister Schofield?' Questioningly he raised his dark eyebrows.

'I...I was just coming to fetch you, Dr Hansford,' Claire managed to reply. 'This is Mrs Hendy—she comes to me regularly to have the dressings changed on her leg ulcer. Mrs Hendy is a diabetic and has medication for a heart condition.'

'Good morning, Mrs Hendy.' Dominic took the notes that Claire handed to him and glanced at them. 'Or may I call you Alice?' he asked a moment later with his devastating smile.

Claire, who was watching Alice Hendy, saw the immediate transformation as her look of suspicion changed to an almost girlish smile.

'You may,' she said. 'I don't really mind my Christian name being used but I do like to be asked first.'

'Do we have any concerns, Sister?' murmured Dominic as he continued perusing the notes.

'The ulcer is healing nicely, Doctor,' said Claire, hoping desperately that no one could hear the rapid beating of her heart, something that always seemed to happen these days whenever Dominic was anywhere near her, 'but there is some swelling around the area which I'd like you to take a look at.'

'I see.' Handing the notes back to Claire, Dominic crouched down in front of Alice and gently began examining the rather taut skin around the ulcer. All that Claire, watching, could think about was how those very hands had touched her, exploring and caressing her own skin so gently and so tenderly. Almost as if he could read her thoughts, Dominic glanced up at her and Claire, in a determined effort to concentrate on what was happening, attempted to pull herself together and put all thoughts of forbidden nights of love right out of her mind.

'I think,' he said, 'you can go ahead and dress the ulcer, Sister, but we do have some oedema there so I will adjust Alice's prescription for her diuretics.'

'Thank you, Doctor,' Claire replied briskly, then, after Dominic had washed his hands and left the treatment room, she set about applying the new dressing to Alice's leg.

'Well,' said Alice with a bemused expression on her face, 'you were certainly right there, Sister. He is nice—very nice, in fact.' She paused. 'How long did you say he's here for?'

'Six months,' Claire replied as she lifted the dressing squares with tweezers and put them in place over the ulcer. Six whole months! How on earth was she going to bear it?

'I wouldn't mind if he stayed,' said Alice with a little grunt.

'That's very fickle of you,' said Claire, forced to smile in spite of the way she was feeling. 'What about poor Dr Lewis?'

'Oh, don't get me wrong,' said Alice. 'Dr Lewis is very nice but just lately, I don't know, he doesn't seem to have had much time for anyone—he seemed so tense all the time.'

'That's one of the reasons he's taking a break,' said Claire, as she began to bandage Alice's leg and to find herself wondering how on earth she would cope if Dominic were to stay at the Hargreaves Centre permanently. Six months was bad enough but at least she could work on the assumption that one day it would come to an end and he would move on out of her life once again. But even that, of course, was in the future, and in the meantime she had to cope with him there, seeing him, being close to him day after day, having him there beside her when she and Mike moved in together as undoubtedly they shortly would.

She had just completed the dressing when Dominic came back into the treatment room with Alice Hendy's amended prescriptions. 'There you are, Alice,' he said, handing her the forms. 'You will see that I've changed the strength of one of your tablets and added a new set to the ones you are already taking. I would like to see you again in a week's time.'

'Thank you very much, Doctor,' said Alice solemnly. 'It's been a pleasure meeting you.'

Alice had barely had time to leave the room, walking very slowly with the aid of two walking sticks, when the intercom sounded and Claire seized the receiver, pleased for any diversion that prevented her from being totally alone with Dominic. It was Sara, one of the receptionists, on the other end.

'Claire?' she said, 'Is Dr Hansford with you?'

'Yes, Sara he is,' she replied.

'Has he finished his surgery?'

'I don't know. I'll ask him.' She turned to Dominic. 'Sara is asking if you have finished your surgery,' she said. When Dominic nodded, she said, 'Yes, he has, Sara.'

'We have a young man here who has come off his bike,' said the receptionist. 'He has quite a deep gash on his forehead which looks as if it might need stitching. Should I send him to A and E or will Dr Hansford see him?'

'Just a minute.' Covering the mouthpiece with her hand, Claire relayed the receptionist's query to Dominic.

'Tell her to send him in,' said Dominic. 'I'll take a look at him before I go out on my house calls.'

'Send him in, Sara,' said Claire. 'Dr Hansford says he will have a look at him.'

There came the sound of a loud sigh from the other end of the line. 'I wish all the doctors were as easygoing as that,' said Sara.

With a tight little smile Claire hung up, turned to begin clearing up, then realised that Dominic was right behind her, so close that if she moved by as much as an inch they would be touching. For a moment she remained very still, hardly daring to breathe, but still he didn't move.

'Dominic…?' she said at last.

'Claire,' he murmured. He was so close she could feel his warm breath on the nape of her neck and for a moment, foolishly, recklessly, she allowed herself to imagine they were back in Rome on that sultry summer's night.

'We need to talk,' he went on eventually, breaking the spell.

'There's nothing to talk about,' she said with a little sigh.

He caught his breath. 'I would say we have everything to talk about,' he said softly. 'I need to talk about the way I feel—I need to hear you talk about the way you feel…'

'But we've said all that,' Claire protested.

'We may have said it once, then,' said Dominic, 'but I need to know how you feel about me now.' Very gently he touched the back of her neck and Claire felt a shiver of desire run down her spine.

'You know the situation now,' she whispered. 'I told you there can be no more between us, that I have Mike…'

'Yes,' he murmured. 'I know all that, but I need to hear you say that you honestly don't feel anything for me now. Can you do that, Claire? Can you?'

She was saved from answering by a sudden tap at the door, and as she turned sharply Dominic moved away from her and Sara came into the room, accompanied by a young man holding a bloodstained towel to his head.

'This is Lee Nicholls,' said Sara. 'He's sixteen years old and he came off his bike and hit his head on a kerb.'

'Hello, Lee.' Dominic moved towards the boy and gently lifted the towel away from his head.

From where she was standing Claire could see that a cut on the side of the boy's forehead was still oozing blood.

'Right,' said Dominic, 'let's have you sitting down.' Gently he led the teenager to a chair and while Sara left the room to return to the reception desk, Claire quickly set up a trolley with equipment to cleanse, tape and dress a wound.

'Is it really bad?' asked Lee, anxiously peering up at Claire from under the towel.

'Nothing that we can't put right,' replied Dominic cheerfully as he pulled on a pair of surgical gloves.

'But there's so much blood.' Lee was looking decidedly pale and Dominic hastened to reassure him. 'We've had worse, haven't we, Sister?' he said, turning to Claire.

'We have indeed,' Claire replied, suspecting that Dominic was referring to Diane and the battle they'd had in trying to control the bleeding from her head wound.

And as she passed swabs to Dominic to cleanse the area his eyes met hers. 'No wet wipes today, Sister?' he asked lightly, and she knew then for sure that he, too, was thinking of that other time when they had worked together. The conditions then had been vastly different from the clinical resources available to them today, but the outcome had depended on each other's professional expertise every bit as much, if not more, as it did now.

Within a few minutes Dominic had applied dressing strips to close the wound and Claire covered it with gauze dressing, which she taped into position before drawing up and administering an antitetanus injection. By the time they had finished, Lee's father had arrived at the centre to take him home.

'Keep an eye on him,' said Dominic. 'There doesn't appear to be any concussion but if he shows signs of excessive drowsiness he will need to go into A and E for an X-ray.'

After Lee and his father had left the treatment room and Claire was clearing away the soiled swabs and empty packaging, Dominic peeled off his gloves and dropped them into the waste bin. 'Talking of Diane…' he said.

'Were we?' Claire raised her eyebrows.

'Oh, yes,' he replied softly, 'I think we both know we were.'

'Well, yes,' she agreed at last, still somewhat reluctant to acknowledge, especially to Dominic, any recollections from that other traumatic time. 'Yes, I suppose we were.'

'I rang the hospital this morning,' he said.

'And…?' Claire allowed her gaze to meet his.

'They have managed to disperse the blood clot,' he replied, 'and they said she had come round briefly.'

'But that's wonderful!' Claire stared at him, all notions of reticence abandoned now in the face of this uplifting news.

'Yes,' he agreed quietly, 'it is. It's still early days, of course, but I managed to speak to Russell and he was very optimistic—there was even talk of flying her home maybe some time next week.'

'He must be so relieved,' said Claire. She paused. 'Was there any news of Ted?' she added.

'Yes, he and May flew home at the end of last week,' said Dominic. 'I imagine he's in hospital in this country now, but he should improve slowly in time.'

'There were times that I really feared for both Diane and Ted,' said Claire slowly. 'I simply didn't think we had the resources to give them the attention they needed…Evelyn, too,' she added. All thoughts of avoiding the subject were abandoned now as once again she and Dominic relived those terrifying moments.

'I know,' he agreed. 'I felt the same way.' He had been fiddling with an empty dressing pack but he threw it down now onto the worktop. 'Claire,' he said urgently, turning towards her, 'we *do* need to talk, you know.'

'Yes,' she agreed helplessly, 'yes, I suppose we do…'

'What we went through was pretty traumatic in itself, without the added involvement of what happened afterwards,' he said.

'I know,' she agreed. 'I did…I did see one of our counsellors here a couple of times and I think I dealt with any post-traumatic stress…'

'Good, but I don't suppose you mentioned the other trauma—the trauma that we went through.'

'Is that what you call it—a trauma?' she said softly, looking up at him.

'Well, it's certainly traumatised me,' he said. A smile played around the corners of his mouth and Claire suddenly had an overwhelming desire to reach up and kiss him. She could have done so quite easily because he was standing so close. All she had to do was to stretch up and…

'So much so,' he went on, 'that I was incapable of returning to the job that I love—the job that once meant the whole world to me.' There was a look of almost helpless desperation in his eyes now.

'We will talk, Dominic,' she said at last, 'I promise you. We will talk and we will try and sort out this thing that happened between us…' She broke off as the treatment-room door suddenly swung open.

Penny came into the room and almost stopped in her tracks as she caught sight of the two of them and gave them a sharp, almost surprised look. 'Oh,' she said, 'I'm sorry—am I interrupting something?'

'No,' said Claire, rapidly pulling herself together, 'of

course not.' She moved smartly away from Dominic and carried on with her clearing up but it wasn't until much later when she was alone that it dawned on her just how close to each other she and Dominic had been standing and of how it must have looked to Penny.

'Claire, darling, I hardly seem to have seen you since you got back from Italy.' It was the following day and Claire was sharing a hurried lunch-break in the staffroom with Mike.

'I know,' she agreed, 'but I did spend a week of that time in Portsmouth.'

'Yes, I know.' Mike bit into a sandwich. 'But even since then it all seems to have been pretty impossible. Tell me, are you free this evening?'

'Er, yes.' She frowned. 'Yes, I think so. What did you have in mind?'

'Well,' Mike considered, 'if I was to pick you up around seven o'clock I thought we could go and have a bite of supper somewhere—just the two of us. I feel we have a lot of catching up to do.'

'That sounds lovely, Mike,' Claire heard herself say. And it would have been lovely once. Before her trip to Italy there would have been nothing she would have liked better than to spend an evening alone with Mike—too often one or both of his children were included and although she didn't mind that, it was nice to have Mike to herself sometimes. So if that was the case, why did she feel so differently now? Why had she been avoiding spending any time with Mike?

She knew the answer, of course. Before her holiday she hadn't met Dominic and now that she had, everything had changed.

She had to sort herself out, she told herself firmly as she sat and watched Mike as he tucked heartily into his lunch, at the same time signing an absolute mountain of repeat prescriptions. She had to forget Dominic and pick up the threads of her relationship with Mike again. It would take a supreme effort to do so, especially as she now had to contend with seeing Dominic day after day, but it had to be done. She couldn't betray Mike any more than she already had, it simply wouldn't be fair to him—he deserved better. He'd been hurt badly enough as it was by Jan when she had walked out on him. She couldn't be the one responsible for putting him through that sort of pain again.

As the thoughts teemed round in her head Mike glanced up, oblivious to her turmoil. 'The new man's settling in well, isn't he?' he said.

'What?' She stared at him, because of the chaotic nature of her thoughts unable to take in what he was saying.

'Dominic Hansford,' he said.

'What about him?' said Claire guiltily.

'I just said he was settling in well,' said Mike, taking a mouthful of coffee.

'Oh, yes. Yes, he is,' Claire replied. 'The patients like him as well,' she added, suddenly desperate to make some sort of intelligent contribution.

'People always like an opportunity for a second opinion,' said Mike with a grimace. 'And it isn't only the patients who are keen on him from what I hear—Christopher was saying something about some ridiculous wager the receptionists are having over who is going to be the first one he asks out—have you ever heard such a thing?'

Claire nodded. 'I know,' she said faintly, 'I heard about that. Poor man, has anyone told him, do you think?'

'I doubt it.' Mike gave a short laugh. 'Not that I have any doubts as to his ability to handle it. I would say Dominic Hansford is more than capable of taking care of himself. He'd have to be,' he went on when Claire remained silent, 'what with all those disaster situations he finds himself in.'

'Yes, quite,' said Claire, then hurriedly, in an attempt to change the subject, not wanting to talk further about Dominic and disaster situations, afraid that somehow the conversation might come round to earthquakes in Italy—which was ridiculous really for there was no way that anyone could connect the two—she went on. 'Tell me, has Emma finished her exams?'

'Yes.' Mike nodded. 'It's Stephen's turn now. Do you know, he…?'

Claire felt her mind begin to wander as Mike began holding forth about his son's recent achievements.

At the end of the day Claire left the Hargreaves Centre and walked home to her flat. It was a warm summer's evening, the air humid and close, full of the distinctive aroma of back-garden barbeques, while the sky overhead was filled with the hum of large aircraft bound for distant parts or returning to London.

Her flat felt hot and stuffy after being shut up all day so the first thing she did on entering was to fling open the windows before running herself a bath. Already she had decided that what was required that evening was a huge effort on her part to put some romance back into her flagging relationship with Mike.

After soaking in the scented water, she carefully applied make-up, painted her nails and brushed her hair, allowing it to hang loose around her shoulders before slipping into the little black dress with the diamanté shoulder straps, knowing it was Mike's favourite but at the same time trying to ignore the fact that it was the one she had worn in Rome. She sprayed herself with a light mist of the French perfume she always wore, stepped into a pair of black high-heeled shoes with jewelled ankle straps and was just searching for the beaded bag that matched her dress when her doorbell sounded.

Mike was early, she thought as she hurried to the intercom. 'Hello?' she said, then went on as he answered with a similar greeting, 'Come on up—I'm nearly ready.'

She had already decided that they would have a glass of champagne before they went out and on her small, glass-topped coffee-table she'd set a bottle to chill in an ice bucket with two glass flutes alongside, while on her CD player romantic music softly played.

She paused for a moment and glanced around the room, determined that tonight should be a success—she owed that much to Mike. What would happen after the meal she had no idea but she didn't want to even think about that now—time enough later to deal with the situation. She wasn't at all sure she wanted Mike to stay the night but, on the other hand, she didn't know how she would dissuade him without hurting his feelings. There came a tap on her door and with a little sigh she crossed the room to answer it.

'You're early, Mike,' she said as she tugged open the door, then she froze, for instead of Mike, Dominic stood on the threshold.

She stared at him, speechless with amazement.

'Hi,' he said, his gaze meeting hers for a long moment before he allowed it to roam over her, taking in every detail of her appearance. 'You look fantastic,' he said at last, and the naked admiration in his eyes was only too obvious. He was wearing a pair of cream chinos and a rust-coloured shirt while his dark hair, without gel, had begun to curl the way it had in Italy.

'I'm going out,' she said stupidly at last.

'I rather gathered that,' he replied. 'I didn't imagine you dressed up like that for an evening in front of the telly.'

'I'm going out with Mike...'

'Yes, I assumed that as well.' He nodded.

'He'll be here in a moment,' she babbled. 'I thought…I thought you were him…'

'Is that why you let me in?' There was amusement in his dark eyes now. 'You really should be more careful, Claire,' he admonished, 'about who you let into your flat—it could have been anyone.'

'Well, yes, quite,' she said coolly, then, taking a deep breath, added, 'Why are you here, Dominic? What do you want?'

'I wanted to talk to you, Claire,' he said. 'It's pretty obvious that we can't talk at work so I thought it might be better if I came round.'

'Well, as you can see, it isn't convenient,' she replied, trying desperately to ignore the fact that her pulse had started to race almost as soon as she had set eyes upon him. 'I really am going out, Dominic, and Mike will be here at any moment—in fact, I don't know quite what I would say to him if he was to find you here…'

'What you're saying is you want me to go, is that right?' He raised his eyebrows.

While she struggled to find a suitable reply her phone suddenly began ringing in the flat behind her.

'Aren't you going to answer that?' he asked, leaning sideways to look over her shoulder into the flat.

'Yes, of course.' Leaving him standing in the open doorway, she crossed to the bookcase and picked up the phone. 'Hello?' she said.

'Claire? Claire, darling, it's Mike.'

'Oh? I was waiting for you.' Her pulse began to race. 'Is everything all right?'

'Claire, I'm so sorry,' he said, 'but I'm not going to be able to make this evening. Stephen has been chosen at the very last moment to play rugby for the school. It's his first time and obviously he's over the moon about it. He's just rung me and he so wants me to be there.'

'What about his mother?' she asked coolly.

'Well, obviously she'll be there as well,' said Mike. 'I'm so sorry, my love, but this really is important for Stephen—I can't let him down. I will make it up to you another time, I promise, and it wasn't as if we were doing anything special, was it?'

She hung up a few moments later and turned to find Dominic watching her carefully. 'Problems?' he said quietly.

'No, not really,' she replied with a shrug.

'That was Mike, wasn't it?' he said.

'Yes, yes, it was.' Suddenly she found it impossible to meet his gaze, hating that he should see her humiliation, her being let down in this way.

'He isn't coming, is he?' said Dominic softly.

'No,' she said. 'No, he isn't.' Sick at heart, she turned away then stopped, her heart suddenly thumping as she realised that Dominic had come right into the flat and had closed the door behind him.

CHAPTER TEN

'WHAT are you doing?' Claire stared at him.

'I know you were anxious for me to go,' he said calmly, 'but that was before, when you thought Mike was going to turn up at any minute. Now we know he isn't coming, I guess there's no urgency.'

'You still shouldn't be here, Dominic.' With a helpless little gesture she turned away again.

'Maybe not.' He shrugged. 'But I'm here now and no one else knows so I can't see it will do any harm.' He glanced around. 'Nice place you have here,' he said admiringly.

'Yes,' she agreed faintly, 'yes, it is. It's a bit small but it suits me.'

'Do you always do that?' he asked suddenly.

'What?' she half turned, her eyes narrowing.

'Have champagne before going on a date?' With his head on one side Dominic was staring with interest at the coffee-table with its ice bucket, glasses and bottle of champagne.

'No, of course not,' she retorted, feeling her cheeks grow hot.

'So, just tonight, then—is that it?'

'Yes, just tonight,' she agreed.

Slowly he allowed his gaze to roam over her, taking in every detail from the little black dress, which in another lifetime he had unfastened and allowed to slip to the floor, to her high-heeled shoes and her hair that gently brushed her shoulders.

'Foolish man, Mike,' he observed drily. 'You dress to look like a million dollars—set a scene like this—and then he ruins it all by not turning up. You wouldn't catch me doing that…'

'Ah, but you don't have two children to consider,' said Claire quickly.

'Maybe not.' Dominic shrugged again. 'But if I had, I think I would have taught them about honouring engagements.'

'You don't understand,' she said, leaping to Mike's defence when, really, deep down she was angry and had no wish to defend him. 'The situation is difficult for Mike. His ex-wife is difficult…'

'I'm sure,' said Dominic, but he sounded far from convinced. 'One good thing, though, is that this gives us that chance to talk that we needed so much.'

'I'm still not convinced that we have anything to talk about,' said Claire stiffly.

'Oh, but we do—' Dominic seemed on the point of explaining but she interrupted him.

'And I'm still not sure that you should even be here,' she added in growing desperation. It was dangerous, having Dominic here in her flat, she knew that. She wasn't at all sure that she could trust either him or herself.

'In that case,' he said calmly, 'I suggest we go out.'

'Go out?' she stared at him stupidly. 'What do you mean, go out?'

'Well, you are all dressed up with nowhere to go,' he replied. 'You obviously haven't eaten and neither have I, so I suggest the next logical step is for us to go out and find somewhere to eat.'

'Oh, I don't think so,' she began, only to have him lift his hand to silence her.

'Come on, Claire,' he protested. 'What possible harm could there be in that? We are colleagues, for heaven's sake, and we do both have to eat.'

'Well...' She bit her lip, wondering if she could dare take him up on his offer.

'Alternatively,' he said, 'we could open that bottle of champagne and maybe send out for a take-away.'

'I think we'd better go out,' she said hastily.

'As you wish.' He inclined his head. 'Right, now we've got that settled,' he went on smoothly, 'where do you suggest we go?'

Rapidly Claire tried to get her brain into gear. Mike, she knew, would have taken her to either the little French bistro on the other side of town or the Indian restaurant in the high street—she decided it was probably better to avoid both of those.

'There's a rather nice-looking Italian restaurant down near the river,' said Dominic, before she had a chance to speak.

'No,' she replied quickly. Italian restaurants were definitely a no-go area as they would be sure to evoke memories for them both that would be far better left alone. 'There's a new wine bar that has just opened opposite the theatre,' she said quickly. 'It also serves food,' she added.

'OK, I'm easy,' he replied. 'Just as long as I get to eat.'

It felt strange, leaving the flat with Dominic and walking through the town to the rather trendy new wine bar. In Italy she would have taken his hand, or at the very least his arm. Now she didn't dare, but it didn't alter the fact that she felt vulnerable and acutely conscious of him by her side, terrified almost that they would be seen together. The wine bar was busy and Claire found herself feeling thankful for that. Maybe it would be easy for Dominic and herself to merge into the crowd. They were given a table tucked away in a corner window, and any initial awkwardness was hidden by Dominic ordering drinks for them both and each of them perusing the menu and ordering their food—a Caesar salad and hot chicken and bacon strips for Claire and steak and salad for Dominic.

'Well, this certainly beats a solitary take-away,' said Dominic as the waiter hurried away with their order and he leaned back in his seat.

'Where are you staying?' asked Claire curiously, suddenly realising that she had no idea where Dominic had been living since coming to Surrey.

'I'm renting an apartment in that old converted brewery near the river,' he replied. 'It's a bit small but it'll serve its purpose.'

'I still don't know why you came,' said Claire in sudden desperation, taking a much larger mouthful than she had intended of her drink and almost choking in the process.

'Yes, you do,' he said quietly, watching her levelly. 'You know exactly why I came.'

'But there was no point, Dominic,' she said in desperation. 'You knew that. I told you, right at the start, I told you about Mike.'

'Yes,' he agreed calmly, 'I know you did, but I happen to believe that something changed—it must have done for you to have slept with me that last night in Rome. Aren't I right?' he said as Claire felt the warm colour flood her cheeks.

'Yes,' she said, 'of course it did. It changed gradually over those few days we were together. Maybe the circumstances helped to bring it about—I don't know—but, yes, it did change.'

'So you must have felt something for me?' He leaned forward, his gaze intense as he sought hers. 'Claire?' he prompted when she didn't immediately answer. 'Can you deny that you felt something for me?'

'No, Dominic, I can't deny it,' she replied at last, 'because if I did it would be a lie. Of course I felt something for you—you know I did. I had to, to have done what I did. I'm not in the habit of going in for one-night stands.'

'I didn't for one moment imagine you were,' he said softly. 'And that's really the reason why I'm here. I don't believe that was a one-night stand any more than you do.'

'But in this case that is exactly what it has to be,' she said desperately. 'In another time and another place it might have been different, Dominic, but because of the way things are between Mike and myself, what happened between us can go no further.'

'Do you love Mike?' he asked suddenly, unexpectedly.

The hesitation was so brief as to be almost imperceptible. 'Of course I do,' she replied, 'otherwise what do you think this is all about?'

'All right.' He nodded. 'But are you *in* love with him?' he added relentlessly.

'What…?' She stared at him.

'Does your heart leap every time you see him?' he asked. 'Does your pulse race and your skin tingle when he touches you?' he went on mercilessly. 'Do you cry out his name when he makes love to you…?'

'Dominic, please!' she protested, throwing a frantic glance over her shoulder.

'You did with me,' he went on in the same soft, unrelenting tone. 'You responded to every move I made. Does he do that for you? Does he love you like that, Claire?'

'Dominic…' She took a deep breath in an effort to steady her nerves. 'Please, don't talk like that…'

'Because if he doesn't make you feel that way,' he went on, ignoring her protests, 'there's no point in going on, Claire, because if you do, take it from me it won't last.'

To her utmost relief she was saved from further embarrassment by the arrival of their food, and while they were eating she made a huge effort and at last managed to persuade Dominic to talk about his work overseas. Inevitably, however, that particular conversation led on to when he would be returning abroad. 'It all rather depends,' he said smoothly, 'on what happens here.'

Very gradually, throughout the course of the meal, Claire felt herself slowly begin to relax. They didn't mention Mike again or her relationship with him; neither did they talk about what had happened between them in Italy. Instead they talked of their families, their respective childhoods and Claire's recent visit to Portsmouth. And then, somehow, the subject came up of Claire's involvement in the stress-counselling clinics run by the Hargreaves Centre.

'Do you enjoy that sort of work?' asked Dominic. They had finished their dessert by now—a raspberry syllabub—and were lingering over coffee.

'Yes, I do,' Claire replied slowly. 'So much so that I have wondered recently whether I should specialise even more in counselling. I have been amazed to find just how much stress is to blame or partly to blame for so many medical conditions.'

He nodded in agreement. 'How often do you take your clinics?' he asked.

'Only once a week at the moment and Penny does the same, but already Richard is wanting us to increase those to two a week each.'

'At that rate he'll be needing to employ another practice nurse,' Dominic observed. 'The centre is incredibly busy.'

'It is,' Claire agreed. 'Mind you, I like it that way. I get bored if I don't have enough to do.'

'Me, too,' he said with a grin.

At last as almost reluctantly they stood up to leave the wine bar Claire was surprised to find that three hours had passed since they had come in. Dominic insisted on paying the bill and Claire instinctively knew it would be pointless arguing with him. It was almost dark as together they strolled back along the riverside path and through the town to Claire's flat. They had fallen silent as they walked as if each had been reminded of the unusual situation they had both found themselves in, and in the end it was Claire who broke the silence as they reached her gate. 'It's been a lovely evening, Dominic,' she said. 'Thank you.'

'Aren't you going to ask me in?' he said softly.

'I don't think so,' she replied, as they stopped at the gate and turned to look up at the little porch at the top of a short flight of steps. 'I really don't think I should.'

'You said you shouldn't have come out with me,' he said, 'but you did, so I can't see another half-hour will make too much difference. Besides, I could do with another coffee.'

Still she hesitated, knowing deep down that letting him into her flat at this time of night could be madness, but at the same time—and probably because of the wine she had drunk with her meal—ready to throw caution to the winds.

'I promise to behave,' he said, making up her mind for her.

'All right,' she replied, rapidly coming to a decision, 'just for half an hour. A quick coffee, that's all.'

'But of course,' he murmured as he followed her up the path. 'What else?'

To her dismay Claire found that her fingers were shaking slightly as she tried to insert her key into the lock, but at last she succeeded and only moments later Dominic was following her up the stairs and into her flat. Leaving him in the sitting room, she immediately headed for the kitchen where she brewed a pot of coffee, which she set on a tray with two china mugs, a small jug of milk and a bowl of sugar.

'Nice,' he said, when she came back and set the tray down on the low table. 'Real coffee.'

'I know you prefer real coffee to instant,' she said without thinking.

'How do you know that?' There was a half-amused expression on his face as he looked up at her from the sofa where he had obviously made himself very comfortable.

'I don't know...' She frowned. 'I must have heard you say some time—either at work or maybe...maybe it was in Italy...'

'Ah, Italy,' he said softly, watching her closely as she poured the coffee. 'We had some good coffee in Italy, didn't we?'

'Yes,' she agreed, 'we did.'

'Do you remember that little street café in the corner of the Piazza Navonna?' he said.

'Yes.' She nodded as he indicated for her to join him on the sofa and, without thinking, she did so. 'And that funny little waiter with the moustache who wanted to practise his English?'

'Of course.' They laughed at the shared memory. 'There were so many things...' he said after a moment.

'Yes,' Claire agreed, 'I was thinking last night...' she went on slowly, then she hesitated.

'Go on,' he said. 'What were you thinking last night?'

'Oh, nothing really...' She shook her head, uncertain now that she should be sharing these thoughts with him.

'No, go on,' he said. 'I want to know.'

'About that little village we went to before...before the monastery.'

'Those wonderful views?' he said.

'Yes,' she said, 'but what I was really thinking about was the quiet...'

'You mean that almost electric feeling in the air?'

'Partly that, I suppose,' she said slowly, 'but also in that little church, the wonderful sense of peace...do you remember that?'

He nodded. 'You could say that was the calm before the storm,' he said quietly. They were silent for a while, each reflecting on individual memories, then Dominic spoke again. 'Isn't it a good thing we can't see what is going to happen?' he said, and when she nodded in reply he went on, 'If we could, we would lead much of our lives in a permanent state of anxiety.'

'You're right,' Claire agreed. 'Just think, if we'd known of the terror that was to come we would never have experienced those wonderful moments of calm because we would have been consumed by dread.'

Reaching along the sofa, he took her hand. 'Were you very frightened?' he asked, his fingers tightening over hers.

'Yes,' she admitted, 'I was terrified. What about you?' She threw him a sidelong glance but didn't withdraw her hand.

'It was pretty scary stuff, wasn't it?' he said with a grimace. 'I have to say, there were a couple of moments when I thought our time was up.'

'You didn't give any indication that you were afraid,' she said. 'You were so calm throughout it all.'

He laughed. 'Put it down to my training,' he said.

'Is your shoulder all right now?' She allowed her gaze to roam to the shoulder that had been injured, the one she had dressed so tenderly.

'It's much better,' he said. 'Still a bit sore at times, but a lot better than it was.'

'It could have been much worse,' she said.

'I know, but I put it down to the fact that I had a good nurse on hand.'

Claire lowered her gaze, suddenly unable to cope with the expression she was seeing in his eyes. 'I hope,' she said quickly, 'the others are all getting on all right. We know about Diane and Ted… But Peter, that was a nasty gash he had on his head… And then there was Nicola, I hope her baby was safe after her ordeal… And Evelyn—do you think she is all right?'

'I'm sure she is,' Dominic replied firmly. 'In fact, I'm sure they all are.'

'There was so little we could do,' Claire went on, 'so few resources at our disposal.'

'I think we improvised very well,' Dominic replied, 'what with your wet wipes, Nicola's T-shirt and your scarf, and I think until my dying day I will carry an image in my head of Archie's triumphant expression as he presented us with those table legs for Ted's splints.'

'I know.' Claire began to laugh. 'And that ward round we did in the dark, stumbling around, bumping into things and tripping over. I'll never forget that as long as I live…'

'It was quite a night, wasn't it?' said Dominic, joining in her laughter. 'What I couldn't believe was how cold it became after that burning sun during the day. It was a good job we had each other to keep us warm…' He trailed off as his eyes met hers and suddenly—and afterwards she wasn't sure quite how it had happened—they were no longer laughing, he had covered the short distance between them on the sofa and she was in his arms.

'Dominic…' she whispered, and then his mouth claimed hers in a kiss so tender, so deep and so passionate that it silenced anything she might have been about to say. It had an inevitability about it, as if they had both been hurtling headlong toward this moment from the very instant he had arrived at the Hargreaves Centre and walked back into her life. It took them back to that one night of bliss that they had spent in each other's arms, reminding Claire, if she had needed any such reminder, of just how good it had been between them.

But in the end it was Claire who drew away, albeit reluctantly, for if she was truthful she knew at that moment that she could have quite happily stayed in Dominic's arms for ever. 'We shouldn't have done that,' she whispered. She turned away from him, only for him to reach out for her again, drawing her back, then taking her face between his hands and lifting it for his kiss.

'I want you, Claire,' he muttered huskily in the moment before his lips covered hers again.

She gave herself up once again to the thrill of being kissed by him but when treacherously her body began clamouring for more, and she knew that he was well aware of that fact, she once again pulled away from him and this time she struggled to her feet. 'This is madness, Dominic,' she protested. 'I knew this would happen—I should never havc let you come in.'

He stared up at her pleadingly for a long moment then he must have seen the tormented confusion in her eyes for with a deep sigh he raked his fingers through his hair then hauled himself to his feet. 'I'd better go,' he said.

'Yes, Dominic, I'm sorry but you had.' In a desperate attempt to get her own feelings under control Claire turned away.

He left immediately, acknowledging her only with a light, almost unbearably poignant touch of farewell on her cheek as he passed her on his way to the door.

In the profound silence after he had gone Claire found her cheeks were wet with tears. She really shouldn't have let him come in, she knew that, just as she knew she shouldn't have gone out with him in the first place. It had been asking for trouble to do such a thing, that was now perfectly obvious. She shouldn't have let herself be seduced by Dominic's talk of there being no harm in it, that they were friends, colleagues. There was no way that she and Dominic could ever just be friends or simply colleagues after what had happened between them in Rome.

Dashing away her tears, she set about clearing up the coffee-tray but while she was still struggling to control her emotions her phone suddenly rang. Wildly, and unreasonably so, she thought it must be Dominic and grabbed the receiver ready in that instant to tell him that she wanted him back, that she didn't care about anyone or anything else, that what they had found in each other was the only thing that mattered.

'Hello?' she said breathlessly.

'Claire?' Her heart sank like a stone. It was Mike.

'Claire, I tried to ring you earlier—where have you been?' he demanded.

'I went out.' Suddenly she felt irritated. Why shouldn't she have gone out, for heaven's sake? Mike had been the one to let her down. What right did he now have to question how she had spent her evening?

'Oh, I see…' As he spoke, Claire realised he wasn't bothered about where she had been and that there was an edge in his tone that was new, an urgency she hadn't heard before. 'Claire, listen,' he said. 'Something's happened. I'm at the hospital.'

'The hospital?' she echoed. 'Why? What is it, Mike, what's happened? Are you all right?'

'It isn't me,' he said. 'It's Stephen—he's had an accident.'

'Oh, Mike!' She was genuinely concerned. 'What's happened? Is he all right?'

'He was injured whilst playing rugby,' said Mike. 'There is concern about the vertebrae in his neck. We are waiting for him to have a scan.'

'Oh, Mike, I'm so sorry. Is there anything I can do? Did you want me to come to the hospital?'

'No, Jan's here with me—it's Emma we are worried about. She was spending the evening at a friend's house. I was ringing to see if you could pick her up.'

'Of course I will,' said Claire immediately. 'Give me the address.'

'It's rather late now,' said Mike, a little huffily Claire thought, 'but I don't suppose it will matter.'

'Do you want me to bring her back here for the rest of the night?' asked Claire.

'No, I've spoken to her,' said Mike, 'and she's adamant that she wants to come here to the hospital.' He went on to give her the address of Emma's friend.

'OK,' said Claire, 'that's no problem. I'll see you shortly.'

Even before she'd hung up Claire had realised she could not drive that night after the few glasses of wine she had drunk with her dinner, but somehow there was no way she could bring herself to tell Mike that. She pressed the disconnect button on her phone then immediately dialled the number of a local taxi firm.

Suddenly she felt consumed with guilt. Just at the time that Mike had needed her most she had been out enjoying herself with another man, and while Mike's son had been lying there in the accident and emergency department of the local hospital, awaiting a scan, she had been here on her sofa in Dominic's arms. What sort of a two-timing woman did that make her, for heaven's sake? Mike didn't deserve this, she told herself severely. He had only ever treated her with kindness and here she was betraying him in the worst possible way—behind his back, and with a colleague at that, which somehow only seemed to make the whole thing even worse.

By the time she had changed out of her little black dress and into jeans, a sweater and a pair of loafers, she had made up her mind to tell Dominic once and for all that it was over between them, that what had happened had been a dreadful mistake and that there could be nothing further in the future. If he chose to remain at the Hargreaves Centre it was his own business, just as long as he understood there could never be anything between them ever again.

CHAPTER ELEVEN

'WHERE have you been? I've been waiting ages!' Emma, eyes red-rimmed, stood with her hands on her hips in the doorway of her friend's house and confronted Claire.

'I wasn't in when your father called,' Claire explained patiently. 'I've only just found out.'

'But where *were* you?' demanded Emma.

'I rather think that is my business,' said Claire, then as the girl's face flushed she went on calmly, 'But I'm here now and there's a taxi waiting so let's not waste any more time.'

Emma maintained a sulky silence for the best part of the journey to the hospital but when they were nearly there she threw Claire a sidelong, apprehensive glance. 'Do you know how bad Stephen is?' she asked.

'No.' Claire shook her head. 'Your dad simply said they were waiting for a scan to see if any damage had been done.'

'He'll probably be all right,' said Emma, but she didn't sound too sure. 'He's always doing silly things and hurting himself. Is my mum there?' she asked as a sudden afterthought.

'Yes, I believe so,' Claire replied. 'I understand she was watching the match with your dad.'

'Good.' Emma nodded then turned her head and gazed out of the car window as they passed a brightly lit shopping mall.

On their arrival at the accident and emergency department of the large county hospital a nurse directed Claire and Emma to the relatives' room where Mike met them. In the room behind him Claire caught a glimpse of Jan who, on seeing Claire, turned away.

'Dad!' Emma hurled herself at her father. 'How's Stephen?' she demanded.

'They've taken him for a scan now,' Mike replied. With his rather crumpled clothes and his hair sticking out at odd angles, he looked even more harassed than usual, which in the circumstances was wholly understandable. Claire's heart went out to him and she longed to give him a comforting hug but something stopped her.

'I want to stay with you and Mum,' said Emma, pulling away from her father and looking past him into the relatives' room.

'Really, you know, it would have been better if you'd stayed with Claire for the night,' said Mike. He spoke in an absent-minded, distracted fashion.

'No!' said Emma. 'I don't want to go with her.'

'Emma, that's very rude,' said Mike, drawing himself up with a start. 'Claire has been good enough to bring you up here—apologise to her this minute.'

'It's OK, Mike,' Claire began uneasily. She was becoming ever more aware of Jan's uncompromising back.

'No,' said Mike firmly, 'it isn't OK. Emma…?'

'Sorry,' mumbled Emma, without looking at Claire. 'But I do want to stay here.'

'All right,' sighed Mike with the air of a man who knew he was beaten. 'Go inside with your mother. I'll be back in a minute. I just want to have a word with Claire.'

Emma disappeared inside the relatives' room and as Jan turned to her daughter Mike shut the door. 'They are very upset,' he said apologetically.

'Of course they are,' said Claire. 'How is it looking, Mike?' she added.

'Not good.' He ran a hand over his hair, smoothing it down. 'I fear there's some damage to his spinal cord.'

'Oh, Mike, I'm so sorry.' Gently Claire touched his arm.

'We won't know for sure until all the tests are complete, but he was in a nasty collision with another lad.'

'Is there anything else I can do?' asked Claire.

'I don't think so,' Mike replied. 'Thanks for bringing Emma up. I had a feeling she would want to be here with us.'

'Do you want me to stay with you?' she asked.

'Well…' His eyes flickered to the closed door of the relatives' room. 'It's a bit awkward…'

'Yes,' she said, 'I know. It's all right, Mike, I do understand and it's only right that Jan should be here with you.'

'Thanks,' he said, but somehow he seemed unable to meet her gaze.

'In that case,' she said, 'I may as well go.'

'I'll phone you in the morning.' Briefly Mike touched her arm.

'Yes, do, please,' she said as he walked to the entrance with her. 'Let me know what is happening.'

By the time Claire had walked across to the waiting taxi Mike had turned back into the hospital foyer and when she glanced back it was to find that he had disappeared.

In spite of the fact that she was exhausted, she barely slept a wink that night as the events of the evening circulated round and round in her brain, and the following morning she staggered in to work hollow-eyed and feeling slightly disorientated.

Under normal circumstances she might have questioned the atmosphere she encountered amongst the girls in Reception that morning—one of frosty, barely concealed hostility. Because of the way she was feeling, however, she let it pass, imagining some squabble over shifts or overtime to be responsible rather than anything directly involving her.

It was Dr Susan Bridges's day off and Claire was to use

her consulting room for her morning of counselling. In a way she was thankful it was a counselling day because that meant little or no contact with Dominic, and in view of the events of the previous evening she was rather glad of that. She would have to face him sooner or later, she knew, but not yet, she told herself wearily.

She was about to press the buzzer for her first patient of the day when her phone rang. It was Sara. 'Claire,' she said, 'I have Dr Naylor on the line for you.'

Once again Claire noticed coolness in the receptionist's tone but she had no time to reflect on it further or to question it because almost immediately Mike's voice came on the line.

'Claire...?' he said.

'Yes. Mike, hello. How is Stephen?'

'He's fractured a vertebra in his neck,' he replied briefly. 'We're going to be staying here with him for the time being,' he added, 'because we don't yet know if there is any further damage to his spine. I've spoken to Richard,' he went on, giving her no opportunity to comment, 'and he's going to divide my surgeries amongst the partners for the next couple of days.'

'Is there anything I can do, Mike?' asked Claire anxiously.

'Er...no, I don't think so,' he replied vaguely. 'I just thought I'd let you know what's happening. I'll ring you again this evening...'

'Yes, all right, Mike.'

'Goodbye, then,' he said.

'Bye, Mike,' she replied. 'Oh, and, Mike,' she said, 'I love you.'

'Oh, yes,' he replied, as if that was the last thing on his mind. Given the circumstances, it probably was. 'Yes, I love you, too.' Then he was gone and for a long while Claire sat gazing at the phone. Did she love him? Or had she just lied because she felt sorry for him and wanted to make him feel better? She really didn't know. All she did know was that if she'd found herself in these same circumstances before going to Italy she would have had no hesitation in answering her own questions but now, because of Dominic, everything had changed and she simply didn't know any more.

With a sigh she pressed the buzzer for her first patient of the day—a woman in her fifties who was being treated by Richard for symptoms of depression, stress and anxiety as a result of taking on too many of the problems of her children, grandchildren and elderly parents. It was not Claire's job to offer solutions to these problems but to listen as the patient talked them through in the hope that she herself might recognise where the difficulties were and in talking about them might be able to see where she could make changes.

That first session lasted a full hour and after it had finished Claire spent a further half-hour entering up notes before sending for her second patient of the morning. This was a young man for whom the demands of his job had simply become too much. He had moved his wife and young family into what he had hoped was a nicer, more rural area but had underestimated the devastating effects that commuting to his job in the city would have on him. He was getting up at five in the morning and not returning home until between eight and nine in the evening. He had coped well to start with, but as he had seen less and less of his wife and children inevitably the strain had started to take effect. He had begun to suffer from insomnia and appetite problems and eventually Dr Bridget Smedley had prescribed antidepressants. In the few sessions he'd had with Claire she had encouraged him to talk things through and see if there was the possibility of adopting an alternative lifestyle to ease his burden.

After this patient had left, Claire was entering up his notes when there came a tap on the door and Dominic entered the room. Her heart turned over, as it invariably did whenever she caught sight of him.

'Dominic,' she said, trying to keep her voice steady, 'I'm in the middle of a clinic.'

'I know,' he replied calmly, 'I just wanted to see if you were all right.'

'Yes,' she said, avoiding his gaze, 'I'm perfectly all right. Why shouldn't I be?'

'I don't know.' He shrugged. 'I heard about Mike's son…and I just wondered, that's all. When did it happen?'

'When I was out with you,' she replied. She allowed her eyes to meet his. 'I feel dreadful about it.'

'Why should you?' He frowned. 'It was hardly your fault.'

'I know, but Mike rang me, thinking I would be at home. He wanted me to pick Emma up…'

Dominic stared at her. 'Well, you weren't to know what was going to happen for heaven's sake,' he said, and there was a touch of exasperation in his tone. 'After all,' he went on, 'he was the one to stand you up, he can hardly expect you to sit around—'

'He didn't stand me up,' she declared hotly.

'No?' he said, raising his eyebrows. 'From where I was standing, it certainly sounded like it.'

'Well, he didn't,' said Claire flatly. 'He simply phoned to say that something had cropped up—Stephen's rugby game—and that he couldn't make it after all.'

'So once again you came second to his family.' Dominic's tone of voice had changed, becoming quieter, but what he had said suddenly angered Claire, probably because deep down she knew what he was saying was the truth.

'I told you—this sort of thing happens,' she said sharply.

'But I accept it. I knew about Mike's family right from the start.'

'Well, you may have accepted it, but I'm finding it very difficult to do so,' said Dominic. 'I might have found it easier if I was utterly convinced that you loved Mike and he loved you, but I'm not.'

'I'm sorry, Dominic, but that's your problem,' she said tightly, feeling her voice begin to rise and her cheeks growing warm. 'After all, I didn't ask you to come here.'

'No,' he agreed, his voice as tight as hers now. 'No, you didn't, and I'm beginning to wonder now exactly why I did.' With that he turned on his heel and strode from the room leaving Claire angrily glaring after him. What was it about this man, for heaven's sake? He either reduced her to a quivering wreck or made her so angry she wanted to scream. Thank goodness no one at the Hargreaves Centre knew about Italy and the devastating consequences of their previous meeting.

Somehow she struggled through the remainder of her clinic until at lunchtime she took herself off to the staff-room. Penny was already in the room, talking to Sara and Carrie as they ate their lunch, but as Claire collapsed in a heap into an armchair the two receptionists stood up and left the room.

'Tell me.' Claire turned to Penny as the door shut behind the two girls. 'What's the matter with those two? Is it something I've said? They were the same this morning when I came into Reception.'

'I think,' said Penny, eyeing her with speculation, 'it's more something you've done than what you've said.'

'But what?' wailed Claire. 'I wish someone would tell me. I can't think of anything...' Suddenly the tensions of the past twenty-four hours threatened to overwhelm her completely.

'Not even going out with a certain dishy locum?' asked Penny.

Claire stared at her. 'Going out with...? I didn't—' she began, but Penny cut her short.

'You were seen, Claire,' she said. 'Jo McMasters saw you last night in that new wine bar with our Dr Hansford.'

'But...but...' Desperately she floundered around for a plausible explanation. 'It was only a spur-of-the-moment thing,' she said at last, 'a chance meeting. He hadn't eaten and neither had I. There was nothing in it, for heaven's sake!'

'That's not what Jo said,' said Penny. 'She said that the two of you were tucked away in a little corner enjoying a meal and that you seemed to be very intimate...'

'We were not intimate!' protested Claire, only too horribly aware that not only had her cheeks flushed but that Penny had seen it and was staring at her with interest.

'Well,' Penny said with a shrug, 'whatever. But that's what Jo said and you know what those girls are like. And let's face it, where Dominic Hansford is concerned... Why, from the moment he set foot in the place,' she went on, 'they've been vying with each other for his attention and they've even had this ridiculous wager going on about which one of the three of them he would ask out first.'

'So that's why they are all so off with me,' said Claire with a sigh.

'Yes.' Penny grinned. 'What they are saying is that it's grossly unfair because you've already bagged one doctor and, not content with that, here you are after another!'

'Oh, for goodness' sake!' said Claire. 'I am not after another! Really, I can't have them going around saying things like that.'

Penny stood up. 'So shall I put them straight, then?' she said. 'I'm going down to Reception now.'

'Yes,' said Claire. 'Yes, please. You can tell them there's

nothing whatsoever between me and Dominic Hansford, that last night was a one-off, and as far as I'm concerned they can keep right on with their bets and their wagers and may the best girl win!'

After Penny had gone Claire found she was shaking. She really couldn't imagine how it had all come to this. If only Dominic hadn't come to the Hargreaves Centre, she told herself angrily, she wouldn't be faced with all these heart-wrenching situations. But the fact was he *had* come and she knew she had no alternative but to simply get on with things, difficult as that might be.

During the next few days tensions seemed to settle down somewhat. The receptionists—no doubt put right by Penny—relaxed and once again began their relentless pursuit of the new locum in the hope that he would eventually notice one of them. Dominic, for his part, seemed oblivious to these ploys and secretly Claire was pleased. She knew she had no right to expect him not to ask anyone else out, but she wasn't at all certain how she would cope with it if he were to do so, especially if it was a colleague. She dreaded the thought of having to see him with someone else and having to witness a romantic relationship unfold in front of her eyes. That it would happen eventually she had little doubt—no one could reasonably expect a man such as Dominic to remain free, unattached and celibate for any length of time. And while she was the one who could change that situation—for he had made that fact plain on more than one occasion—she also knew she was powerless to do so.

Mike was in such a fragile and vulnerable position Claire knew she could not do anything that might in the slightest way add to his distress. He continued to spend the best part of each day at the hospital at his son's bedside while he and Jan and Emma waited to see the results of the many tests the boy had undergone. Claire herself didn't return to the hospital again, feeling her presence there would simply be an intrusion, speaking instead to Mike each evening on the phone. Somehow his partners and the rest of the staff coped with the increased workload that his absence had created.

But for Claire the most difficult aspect of those days was the coolness that had sprung up between herself and Dominic since the heated words they had exchanged on the morning after Stephen's accident. He made no further attempt to come to her flat and no longer sought her out at work. When they did meet he was polite but cool and rather distant, and while this was precisely the way she had indicted that things should be between them, inside her heart was breaking. And at night when she was alone it was agony because in those lonely, dark, small hours before dawn she was forced to confront her demons and to admit that deep down in her heart she knew she loved Dominic.

There was no telling how long things might have carried on in this way if something hadn't happened which was to change everything.

It was towards the end of the week, when Claire was taking a clinic for Dominic and had just seen the last patient. 'Everything all right, Sister Schofield?' asked Dominic, inspecting the dressing she had just applied.

Still there was that coolness in his tone that almost tore Claire apart, but she knew there was nothing she could do to change it. Any sign of weakening on her part might be seen by him as encouragement, and she couldn't risk that happening because she knew if it did there was a very good chance that she might not be able to resist him for a second time. 'Everything is fine, Dr Hansford,' she replied briskly. 'Would you sign the prescriptions, please, while I finish here?'

'Of course.' As he turned away to sign the patients' prescriptions the treatment-room phone suddenly rang.

Claire picked up the receiver. 'Hello?' she said.

'Oh, Claire.' It was Sara, and Claire allowed herself a rueful smile at the girl's friendly tone—a far cry from a few days previously when she had suspected that Claire and Dominic might be an item. 'Have you finished your clinic?'

'Almost,' Claire replied with a quick glance at Dominic, who was still signing prescription forms. 'Why, do you have someone else for me?'

'Not exactly,' Sara replied. 'But there is someone here in Reception to see you.'

'All right, Sara,' Claire replied. 'I'll be out in a moment. Do you know who it is?'

'No, they didn't say, but I don't think they are registered here.'

'All right.' Claire replaced the receiver and after Dominic had given the forms to their patient she helped the woman to her feet and escorted her to the door.

'I have to go to Reception,' she said to Dominic. 'Apparently there is someone waiting to see me.'

'I'll come with you,' said Dominic. 'I need the girls to search for some records for me.'

Together they left the treatment room and in silence walked down the corridor to Reception. Claire's heart was heavy and suddenly she longed for the old easy way there had been between them but which now seemed to have disappeared for ever.

Afterwards she found it difficult to remember the exact sequence of events because the element of surprise was so total, but at the time as she and Dominic entered Reception she remembered seeing that Mike was there. She imagined he must have come in briefly maybe to simply touch base and pick up his mail. All the reception staff were there also, busily tidying up after the morning surgeries, and Penny was there, talking to Christopher as he sorted out his house calls.

Claire turned to the waiting area to see who it was who was waiting to see her and there, sitting there side by side, looking almost exactly as they had done in Italy, in floral-printed, summer dresses and white cardigans, were Dorothy and Evelyn.

The shock was so great that momentarily Claire was speechless and it was Sara who spoke first. 'Claire,' she called, leaning over the desk, 'these ladies have come to see you. One of them says you helped to save her life in Italy…' She trailed off as it became apparent that no one was listening to her. Claire had moved forward as if in a dream. Evelyn had risen to her feet and, reaching out, clasped both of Claire's hands in hers, but it was from her sister Dorothy that the loud cry of surprise came.

'Dominic!' she cried, and everyone in reception turned towards them. 'Dr Hansford!' Excitedly Dorothy turned to her sister. 'Evelyn,' she said, 'look who's here! We didn't expect this, did we? We knew you worked here, Claire…' she turned to Claire '…because May told us, but we had no idea we would find Dominic here as well.'

'Well!' Evelyn turned from Claire to Dominic, her face flushed with pleasure. 'That's wonderful! Now we can thank both of you!' She turned towards the desk where Sara and the other receptionists were staring open-mouthed, where Mike had paused in what he was doing to look in mild surprise at the little group in the waiting area and where Penny had stopped in mid-sentence in her conversation with Christopher and was staring at Claire with an expression on her face which implied that the last piece of a puzzle which had previously eluded her had finally fallen into place.

'Do you know,' said Evelyn to everyone in general,

blissfully unaware of the impact that their visit was causing, 'if it hadn't been for these two wonderful people in Italy I wouldn't be here today—and I'm not the only one either,' she went on when no one spoke, 'because, I can tell you, there are several others who owe their lives to them as well.'

CHAPTER TWELVE

'SO, ARE you going to tell me what this is all about?'

It was later, much later, and Penny had come into the treatment room where Claire was alone and had shut the door behind her.

'I don't really know where to begin,' said Claire helplessly. The afternoon seemed to have passed in a sort of blur since that heart-stopping moment in Reception and she was still feeling rather disorientated. She and Dominic had taken Dorothy and Evelyn to the staffroom where they had given them tea and biscuits before the two sisters had carried on their journey to Guildford where they were to look up an old school friend.

'It seemed too good an opportunity to miss, being so close to the Hargreaves Centre,' Dorothy had said. 'We so wanted to see you again and to say thank you.'

Claire doubted they would ever know the havoc they had caused.

'How about starting at the beginning?' said Penny now.

'You mean in Italy when Dominic and I first met?' asked Claire wearily. All she had really wanted to do was to go home, go to bed and pull the duvet over her head, shutting out everything—the expressions on the receptionists' faces, surprise turning to suspicion as the truth became apparent, the bewilderment on Mike's face, and the prospect of all the questioning and explaining she knew lay ahead. Maybe, though, Penny was a good place to start. Penny was her friend and hopefully would be on her side.

'Yes,' said Penny, 'if you like. But one thing first, something that is really bugging me.'

'Yes?' Claire gave a little sigh, knowing only too well what was coming.

'Why didn't you let on that you knew Dominic when he first came to the centre?' asked Penny curiously.

'I couldn't.' Claire shook her head.

'But why not?' Penny frowned.

'Because of Mike,' said Claire simply.

Penny stared at her for a long moment. 'Ah,' she said at last, 'are you saying what I think you're saying?'

'Yes, Penny.' Claire briefly closed her eyes. 'I guess I am.'

'So maybe Jo McMasters wasn't so far off the mark after all with what she saw in the wine bar.' When Claire remained silent Penny took a deep breath. 'OK,' she said at last, ' let's go back to the beginning again. Did you get to know him before the earthquake or was it because of the earthquake?'

'Well,' Claire said consideringly, 'sort of before, but then afterwards, of course, the earthquake changed everything.'

'Tell me about before,' said Penny.

'We were staying at the same hotel.'

'Did he chat you up?' Penny was half smiling now and as Claire remembered the scene by the Trevi fountain she suddenly felt indignant.

'No,' she said quickly, 'of course not!'

'So he didn't fancy you, or you him—not even just a little bit?' Penny's gesture between her thumb and forefinger indicated a tiny amount.

'Well...I don't know really,' Claire floundered, then with a deep sigh she said, 'I suppose if I'm honest, I found him attractive from the very beginning.'

'Well, yes, quite,' said Penny, her tone matter-of-fact now. 'I mean, who wouldn't with those devastating dark looks? Why, the man positively smoulders!'

'Yes, well,' Claire went on hurriedly, 'there was a crowd

of us, you see, and we joined up for meals and drinks and things.'

'A bit like these 18 to 30 clubs you hear about?' asked Penny. She spoke innocently enough but Claire detected a wicked glimmer in her eye.

'No! No,' said Claire hastily, 'nothing like that at all. Why, one couple were there to celebrate their golden wedding...'

'So, more like an old folks outing, then, what with those two old dears that came in today?' said Penny, and once again the wicked gleam was back in her eyes.

'No,' said Claire almost in exasperation now, 'it wasn't like that either. There was, in fact, a very good age mix. There were several couples around our age. There was even one couple on their honeymoon...'

'All couples, then?' asked Penny. She spoke casually but Claire knew what she was driving at.

'No,' she said firmly, 'there was a young man on his own—a student actually. His name was Archie...'

But Penny didn't seem particularly interested in hearing about Archie. 'So tell me about you and Dominic,' she said.

'Well, we seemed to hit it off straight away,' said Claire warily. 'Maybe it was because of the shared medical thing—I don't know.' She shrugged. 'But we just seemed to get on. Mind you, that happens on holiday, doesn't it? It always seems easy to talk to strangers. I mean, let's face it, you don't know anything about them and they don't know anything about you—they haven't heard all your stories before and you haven't heard theirs...'

'Get on with it, Claire,' said Penny.

'What?' Claire glanced sharply at Penny then, catching sight of her expression, said, 'Oh, right, well, like I was saying, we seemed to get on really well. Anyway, we both signed up for the Assisi trip, together with the rest of the group from the hotel.'

'Did Dominic know about Mike at this point?' Penny interrupted curiously.

'Yes,' Claire replied. 'I told him about Mike right at the beginning.'

'Why did you do that?'

'I felt I had to.'

'So you recognised that there could have been something between you from the very start?'

Claire only hesitated for a moment before replying. 'Yes,' she said quietly, knowing there was no earthly point in trying to fool Penny any longer, 'I knew and so did he. That was why I had to be totally honest with him.'

'Does he have anyone in his life?'

'He said not.' Claire shook her head. 'I must say I found it hard to believe,' she added slowly, 'an attractive man like that, but in the end I put it down to the life he'd led. He told me all about the work he'd done in various parts of the world with children's charities and he more or less said that he wasn't in any one place long enough to make any sort of lasting commitment.'

'So what happened next?'

'We went on the Assisi trip and got caught up in the earthquake. Things changed then,' she said slowly. 'It's very hard to explain but Dominic and I got thrown together even more. For a start we were the only ones with real medical knowledge, but the people we were treating weren't strangers—they had become friends by then and it was all terribly difficult… I really can't go into it all again, Penny. I still find it very upsetting, wondering if we could have done more…' She broke off.

'OK,' said Penny calmly. 'What about afterwards?'

'What do you mean, afterwards?' Claire threw Penny an uneasy glance.

'Well, when you got back to Rome, did you come straight home after that?'

'No,' Claire swallowed. 'We stayed on for a few days.'

'Did everyone do that?'

'No,' Claire replied. 'Only Dominic and me.'

'Ah,' said Penny, 'so is that what this is all about—what happened after you returned to Rome?'

'Yes,' said Claire in a small voice, 'I suppose it is. You see, I was pretty upset over all that had happened, and Dominic, well, he was shaken, I suppose, by the events, although he was more used to dealing with traumatic situations like that than I was. But we both felt we needed some time and space to sort ourselves out before returning to England.'

'But none of the others felt that way?'

'No.' Claire shook her head. 'I guess it was different for them because although they had injuries to deal with they didn't have emotional trauma to cope with...' She paused. 'Apart from one couple who had been hoping the holiday would patch up their shaky marriage.'

'And did it?' asked Penny.

'She was badly injured—remember the one I told you about with the severe head injury who later developed a blood clot? But, yes, actually, I think the whole dreadful experience may have brought them together again.'

'Sometimes it takes something like that...' said Penny thoughtfully. 'Do you know what their problem was?' she added.

'He'd had an affair, she was finding it difficult to forgive him and he was still missing the girlfriend who had since met someone else and had a baby.'

'Heavens—the games people play,' said Penny, rolling her eyes. 'But you say you felt the experience might have brought them closer?'

'I hope so. He was certainly devastated when he thought he might lose her,' said Claire.

'So, getting back to you and Dominic,' Penny went on, 'what happened next?'

Claire took a deep breath. 'I slept with him,' she said bluntly. 'Only the once,' she said when she caught sight of Penny's expression. 'I couldn't help it,' she added. 'I couldn't bear the thought that I would never see him again.'

'And you thought sleeping with him might make that easier?' asked Penny wryly.

'Yes, I suppose I did.' Claire's voice was barely more than a whisper.

'And did it?' Penny raised one eyebrow.

'In one way,' Claire said, 'because it gave me a wonderful memory that I can draw on…but, no, in another way it simply made things worse because I knew it could never happen again. I told him that at the time,' she explained, suddenly desperate that Penny should understand the situation and not believe the worst of her, 'I told him that I could never see him again—that I was committed to Mike and that we would shortly be moving in together.'

'And did he accept that?'

'At the time I thought he had,' Claire replied. 'I came home and tried to get on with my life…'

'How did you feel?' asked Penny curiously. 'I know you were rather stressed out but I thought that was all due to the experience you'd been through.'

'Well, yes, and it was, partly,' Claire explained, 'but I felt terrible at leaving Dominic and I found I couldn't cope with the fact that I might never see him again. And then when I saw Mike I felt so guilty… When Mike said I had to take some time off, at first I didn't want to but then, I confess, I couldn't wait to get away. I thought if I went to my father's for a while I might be able to get my head straight, and to a certain extent, I suppose I did.' Claire frowned. 'I certainly felt a bit better when I came back to work—but then, when I found Dominic here, it was a tremendous shock and I was right back at square one again.'

'What I can't understand,' said Penny slowly, 'was how he came to be here. How did he know we wanted a locum?'

'I'd told him,' said Claire ruefully. 'Right back at the beginning when we first met, we were talking about our jobs. I told him I worked here and that one of our partners was going on sabbatical. I apparently mentioned we would be replacing him with a locum.'

'Did he indicate he was looking for a job at that time?' asked Penny with a frown.

'No.' Claire shook her head. 'Not at all. He said he'd been working at an A and E department in this country because his father had been ill but that soon he would be returning abroad.'

'But he came here instead,' mused Penny.

'I think he thought I would change my mind about staying with Mike,' said Claire. 'I told him I couldn't,' she went on quickly. 'I had committed myself to Mike and he knew that. I can't hurt Mike, Penny. Heaven knows, you know what he went through when Jan left him. I can't be responsible for putting him through that again—and especially now when he is so worried and upset over Stephen…'

'Hang on a minute.' Penny held up her hand, stopping Claire in mid-flow, 'I think there are a few things we need to get straight here.'

'What do you mean?' Claire stared at her.

'Well, for a start, have you not heard the news on Stephen today?'

'No. What?' Sudden fear gripped Claire's heart.

'He's out of danger,' said Penny, 'and apparently there's no permanent damage to his spine. He'll be fine again when the fracture heals.'

'Oh,' said Claire, relief flooding over her. 'How do you know?'

'Mike said so. That was what he'd come in to tell us today. I'm sure he would have told you, but you went off with Dominic and your two old ladies...'

'Oh, no!' said Claire. 'I had no idea. But that's wonderful news—about Stephen. They must be so relieved—all of them.'

'Well, yes, absolutely,' said Penny. 'But coming back to you and Mike, honestly, Claire, I really do think you have to come clean with him.'

'Oh, Penny, I can't.' Claire stared at her friend in anguish. 'I told you I can't bear to see him hurt again and to know that I would be the one responsible for doing it.'

'Claire, listen to me.' Stepping forward, Penny took hold of Claire's shoulders. 'Are you in love with Dominic?'

'Well, I don't know... I suppose... I can't really...'

'Are you in love with him?' Penny repeated, ignoring Claire's ineffectual dithering.

Helplessly Claire stared at her. 'Yes,' she whispered at last, 'yes, I guess I must be.'

'Right.' Penny gave a huge sigh and let go of Claire. 'At last we're getting somewhere. Now,' she went on after a moment, 'the next thing is, you have to tell Mike. Oh, I know you say you can't bear to be the one to hurt him for a second time,' she went on when she caught sight of Claire's expression, 'but don't you think that is exactly what you will be doing in the long run if you stay with him, knowing that you are in love with someone else?'

'Come on, Claire,' Penny urged when Claire remained silent, 'think about it. If you stay with Mike now and maybe eventually marry him, it would be an absolute disaster. You can't do that to him. Mike's a decent guy. You simply can't be that cruel. You have to tell him, hard as that might be.' She paused. 'Mind you,' she added drily, 'telling Mike could be a doddle compared to telling those girls in

Reception. I wouldn't want to be in your shoes when you tell *them* that you and the devastating Dominic Hansford are an item.'

Claire spent a night of turmoil as she went over and over in her mind all that she had discussed with Penny. In the end, just as dawn was breaking, she finally came to a decision and knew what she had to do. After that she managed to sleep, even though it was only for a couple of hours, but because it was Saturday, luckily, she did not have to go in to the centre.

After she'd showered and dressed, drunk some fresh orange juice and nibbled a piece of toast, she was preparing to leave the house to drive across town to the small terraced house that Mike had moved into after the break-up of his marriage when she opened the outer door, to be confronted by Mike himself who was on the point of ringing her doorbell.

She stared at him in amazement. 'Mike!' she exclaimed. 'I was just on my way to see you.' He looked exhausted and as she recalled the ordeal he had just been through her heart went out to him. 'I wanted to talk to you,' she said. 'But what are you doing here?' she added curiously.

'I wanted to talk to *you*,' he said. 'Can I come in?'

'Yes, of course.' She stood aside, letting him into the large hallway before shutting the front door behind him. In silence she led the way up the stairs to her flat, all the while her mind racing. Why had he come? She'd had everything so carefully rehearsed in her mind, but his sudden and unexpected arrival had thrown her and she couldn't think now what she had planned to say to him.

'I heard about Stephen,' she said at last, leading the way into her sitting room and breaking the silence between them, which was threatening to become unmanageable. 'Penny told me. It's wonderful news, Mike. I'm so pleased.'

'Yes,' he said, 'it was a tremendous relief to know there was no permanent spinal damage. He's not entirely out of the woods yet but I think it's just a matter of time. He's young...he'll mend.' As he was talking he was looking around the flat, as if he'd never been there before, never seen any of her possessions or furniture, which was ridiculous when one considered just how many times he *had* been there.

'Can I get you anything, Mike?' asked Claire in sudden desperation. 'Coffee perhaps or fruit juice?'

'No,' he said quickly, 'no. Maybe later, but I...we need to talk first...'

'Is this about yesterday?' she asked wildly, unable to bear the suspense any longer.

'Yesterday?' Mike looked blank.

'Yes, because I wasn't around when you came in to tell us about Stephen? I'm...I'm sorry about that, Mike,' she rushed on, 'but, you see, those two ladies had turned up...they were people I'd met in Italy...they were caught in the earthquake...and there are other things about that, about Italy, that I need to tell you...'

'Oh, yes,' said Mike vaguely. 'Someone said something about those ladies and you helping to save lives...'

'So isn't that why you're here?' Claire frowned. She'd imagined that, like Penny, he'd by now have put two and two together where she and Dominic were concerned.

'No.' He took a deep breath. 'That isn't why I'm here, Claire. Do you mind if I sit down?' he said.

'No, of course not. Please...' She indicated the sofa and as Mike sank down, almost as if his legs were in danger of giving way, Claire also sat down, opposite him, perching apprehensively on the arm of an easy chair.

'Claire, I don't know how to say this,' he began. Running his hands through his hair, he attempted to go on, 'You see, in the past week or so, since Stephen's accident, something has happened, something which I never ever imagined would happen. If I had thought there was the slightest chance I would never have allowed our relationship to reach the stage it did. You came to mean so very much to me, Claire…but you see…the children…I hadn't realised, neither had Jan really…' He trailed off helplessly as if it was impossible for him to find the words he wanted.

'What are you saying, Mike?' Claire stared at him in astonishment.

'I'm sorry, Claire,' he said, and there was a look of real anguish on his face. 'So very sorry, I really am. The last thing I wanted was to hurt you. In fact, I have been desperate not to hurt you…'

'Mike, are you trying to say that you and Jan…?'

He nodded fearfully, hardly able to meet her gaze, 'I know I always said it would never happen, that I would never under any circumstances take her back, but something happened during those dreadful days at Stephen's bedside and we finally began to realise just what we had thrown away. We…' He gulped. 'We have decided…that we are going to try again and have another go at our marriage. Honestly, Claire,' he appealed to her, 'I really am so very, very, sorry…'

'But I think that's wonderful, Mike,' said Claire softly.

'Like I say,' he carried straight on, almost as if he hadn't heard her, 'the last thing I wanted was to hurt you.' He broke off as if it had just dawned on him what she had said. 'What did you say?' His eyes narrowed in bewilderment as he looked at her.

'I said I think it's wonderful,' she said. 'Wonderful that you and Jan are going to have another go at marriage and especially wonderful for Stephen and Emma—they must be over the moon.'

'Yes, but…what about you?' He frowned, shaking his head. 'Aren't you upset, Claire?'

'A bit,' she admitted, 'because at one time I'd hoped our relationship was going to be long-lasting, but let's just say not so much as I might have been a few weeks ago.'

'I don't understand.' He stared at her, looking thoroughly puzzled now.

'You s-see, Mike,' she said, stumbling over her words slightly as it slowly dawned on her that what she had been dreading might not now be anywhere near as bad as she had feared, 'I also have someone else in my life...'

He continued staring at her. 'You have someone...?'

'Yes, Mike,' she said softly, and as she looked at him and he at her she gradually saw something change in his expression, some recognition of her as if he was seeing her properly for the first time in a very long time.

'It's Dominic Hansford, isn't it?' he said slowly at last. He spoke in the manner of someone who had been vaguely aware of something for some time but who had been unable to put his finger on what it was.

'Yes,' Claire replied quietly, 'it's Dominic.'

'Someone said you met him in Italy...'

'That's right, I did,' she agreed. 'But I didn't know he would seek me out, that he would come to the centre. Mike, you have to believe that.'

'OK.' Mike still looked rather shell-shocked, 'I must admit I did wonder when I heard that you'd met in Italy why neither of you had let on.'

'I was annoyed with Dominic for following me when I had made it quite plain that we could have no future together,' said Claire slowly, 'and I suppose I kept the whole thing quiet because of you, Mike,' she added.

They were silent for a moment, as if each was digesting what they had just learnt, then Claire spoke again. 'I didn't want you to be hurt,' she said, 'and I didn't feel there was any need for you to know about something that I believed by then was over.'

'Only it wasn't over, was it?' said Mike, his gaze meeting hers.

'No...' she hesitated. 'It wasn't. I'm sorry, Mike.'

'Don't be sorry,' he said, leaning forward and taking her hand. 'Maybe we should both be thankful that we've recognised what we want before it was too late.' He paused. 'You said you were coming to see me, Claire. Were you coming to tell me about you and Dominic?'

'Yes.' Claire curled her fingers around his hand and squeezed it tightly. 'It was Penny who made me see that it wouldn't be fair to anyone if I went on living a lie.'

'That's quite right,' Mike agreed, then after a moment, he said, 'Does Dominic know any of this?'

'No, not yet.' Claire shook her head. 'He is still under the impression that I am working at my relationship with you.'

'In that case, don't you think you should go and see him right now and put the poor man out of his misery?' said Mike softly.

'Oh, yes,' said Claire. 'Yes, I will.'

The old brewery building, which had recently been tastefully converted into modern apartments, stood on a bend in the river. In the past this had been a busy stretch of water with many merchants' vessels taking goods to the nearby port. Now it was a comparatively quiet backwater, its moorings filled with houseboats and cabin cruisers.

There was little or no breeze that morning and warm, hazy sunshine, which sparkled on the water. A family of ducks trailed downstream, the ripples behind them forming a wide V-shaped wedge while two swans glided effortlessly around the moored boats. Claire saw Dominic before he saw her so had the advantage of being able to study him unobserved for a while. He was talking to the owner of a particularly colourful houseboat, the glossy sheen of its black woodwork decorated with garlands of brightly painted flowers. Casually dressed this morning in faded blue denims and a black, ribbed vest-style shirt, his hair looked wet, as if he'd just stepped out of the shower.

Claire hadn't really seen him since the previous day when together they had entertained Evelyn and Dorothy in the staffroom. After the two ladies had taken their leave Dominic had thrown her a wry glance. 'It rather looks,' he'd said, 'as if the cat might be out of the bag now, doesn't it?'

She had only been able to agree with him, at that moment fearful what effect the sisters' visit might be about to have on their lives. Since then, of course, everything had changed—she still could hardly believe by just how much. Now, as she stood there watching Dominic her heart suffused with love for this man who had entered her life in such a dramatic way and who had since, quite literally, turned her world upside down. She had believed herself to have been in love with Mike, and in her way she had loved him and at the time it had been very real, but that had been before she had known what it was to have loved and to have been loved by Dominic. After that it had seemed that nothing could ever be the same again.

As if he sensed someone watching him, he half turned, and when he saw her standing there he straightened up, murmured something to the man on the boat and slowly began walking towards her.

'Claire…?' he said wonderingly when he was close enough to read the expression in her eyes. 'This is a surprise…'

'I need to talk to you, Dominic,' she said softly.

'Really…?' He frowned for a moment, trying to read what was in her eyes, then—with a quick glance back at the man on the houseboat, who was eyeing Claire with interest, and a second glance up at the old brewery where he now lived—he said, 'Why don't we take a walk?'

'Yes,' she said, 'that would be nice.' She could tell he was apprehensive about what she was going to say, why she should have sought him out on a Saturday morning. Together they began to stroll along the towpath beneath a belt of willows whose branches formed a cool, green tunnel, the tips of their leaves trailing in the water, then out on the other side to where the river meandered gently through lush water-meadows thick with clusters of yellow musk and huge white daisies.

'Has the balloon gone up?' asked Dominic at last, casting her a sidelong glance.

'How do you mean?' She hesitated, unsure now how to tell him, not wanting him to think she had only come to him because Mike had left her.

'Well, I imagine after Dorothy and Evelyn left, Mike wanted some answers,' he said with a wry smile.

'There was certainly some explaining to do,' Claire agreed, 'but it wasn't Mike who wanted the explanation—it was Penny.'

'Penny?' Dominic looked mildly surprised.

Claire nodded, 'Penny and I have been friends, close friends, really, ever since I came to the Hargreaves Centre,' she said, 'and I would say she knows me pretty well. She had already picked up on something since my return from Italy and especially since you came here to work, but I don't think she could quite put her finger on what it was. Anyway,' she went on when he remained silent, 'when Dorothy and Evelyn turned up and let on that we had all been in Italy together, Penny immediately wanted to know why I hadn't mentioned that fact when you first arrived at the centre.'

'And what did you tell her?' There was a glint of amusement in his dark eyes now.

'I told her I hadn't been able to say anything because of Mike,' Claire replied quietly. 'She, of course, then immediately put two and two together and realised that we must have meant something to one another in Italy.'

'Well, yes.' Dominic considered for a moment. 'I guess that's putting it mildly, but, yes, I suppose she was on the right track. So, did you deny this fact or admit it?' he asked curiously.

'I admitted it,' said Claire.

He stopped, taking her hand as he did so and tugging it slightly so that she, too, was forced to stop and face him on the narrow towpath. At this point on the pathway the cow parsley grew so high it obscured them from anyone passing on the river. It was quiet, so quiet that the only sounds to be heard were the buzzing of a bee as it darted from one flower to another and the occasional plopping sound from the water as fish came up for the insects that skimmed the surface. 'What did you admit?' he said softly, looking down into her eyes.

'That I fell in love with you in Italy,' she said, 'but that I felt I had to forget you when I came home because I didn't want to hurt Mike.'

'And what did Penny have to say about that?' he asked.

'She said I would end up hurting everyone if I carried on the way I was,' Claire replied simply.

'Clever lady, your friend Penny,' observed Dominic. Gently drawing her towards him, he tilted her chin, dropped a kiss on her forehead, then another on the tip of her nose.

'I really had thought I loved Mike,' said Claire, 'but that was before I met you...'

'So are you going to tell him now?' he asked, urgently searching her face.

'I already have,' she said.

'You have?' There was no disguising the light that flared in his eyes.

'Yes.' Claire took a deep breath. 'I made up my mind that I was going to see him this morning,' she explained. 'I was going to tell him everything. But even before I had the chance to leave the house he came round to see me.'

'How did he take it?' asked Dominic.

'Not as badly as I feared,' said Claire with a little sigh. 'You see, what he had come to tell me was that he and his ex-wife Jan are going to give their marriage another try...'

'You're joking!' Dominic stared at her.

'No.' She shook her head. 'It appears that while they werc at their son's bedside while he was so ill they were drawn together again.'

'Amazing,' said Dominic, 'although, now I think about it, I can't say I'm that surprised. Mike still seemed very involved with his family and his ex-wife certainly didn't appear to have let go.' With a sudden grin, he said, 'Does this mean we can shout our love from the rooftops now?'

'Well, I don't know about that...' Claire began.

'I do love you, you know, Claire,' he said urgently, suddenly growing serious again. 'I still can hardly believe it, but that's the way it is. Before I met you I had convinced myself I wasn't ready to settle down or form any lasting relationship, but that all changed that week in Italy. The moment I set eyes on you I knew you were the one for me and after the experience we went through I was even more convinced.'

'I know,' she whispered. 'It was the same for me. What happened was truly amazing.'

'I know I shouldn't have followed you and come to work at the centre,' Dominic went on, 'but I couldn't help myself, Claire—you have to believe that. I couldn't just let you go. I knew I was in love with you and I felt deep down, in spite of what you had said about it having to end, that you felt the same way about me.' As he spoke he slipped his arms around her waist, drawing her towards him again.

'You were right,' whispered Claire. Reaching up, she wound her arms around his neck and with a little sigh of bliss allowed her fingers to sink into his dark hair, something she had been longing to do ever since that night in Rome.

'I love you, Claire,' he murmured, his voice husky with desire. 'I love you and I want you to be my wife.' She was unable to reply as his mouth covered hers at that moment in a kiss that awakened all the love and passion that had simmered below the surface since they had parted.

When at last they drew apart he looked questioningly into her eyes. 'Claire?' he murmured. 'Will you marry me?'

'Oh, yes,' she said with a deep sigh. 'Yes, with all my heart.'

Together they turned and with arms entwined made their way back along the riverbank past the row of houseboats and into the old brewery where they climbed the stairs to Dominic's apartment.

EPILOGUE

'IT WORKED, didn't it?' Dominic said.

'What?' Claire murmured dreamily as she lifted her face to the cooling spray from the fountains.

'Our coins,' he replied. 'I told you two coins in the fountain would ensure our return to Rome, didn't I?'

'Yes,' she agreed, putting up her hand to shield her eyes from the hot Italian sun, 'you did, but even you couldn't have foreseen that our return would have been on our honeymoon.'

'Oh, I don't know,' he said with a lazy smile, that same smile that still turned Claire's heart over every time she saw it. 'I wanted you the moment I set eyes on you and I guess I simply made up my mind there and then.'

'That's quite shocking, Dominic Hansford,' she reproved mildly.

'So didn't you want me?' he asked, raising one eyebrow.

'Of course not!' she protested. 'I don't go around looking at strange men and deciding I want them there and then.'

'I hope you don't,' he said. 'At least not now, but what about then?' he added. 'Can you honestly say that you didn't feel anything that day we first spoke here by the Trevi?'

'Well, I suppose I might have done,' said Claire with a little pout.

'What did you feel?' he murmured, moving closer to her and gently caressing the back of her neck with his thumb. 'Go on, tell me, I want to know. What did you feel?'

'Attraction?' she said, half turning her face towards him as her senses responded to his touch.

'Is that all?' He sounded mildly disappointed. 'Attraction? Is that the best you can do? What about desire? Didn't you even feel the first stirrings of desire?'

'Well...' She pretended to consider. 'I guess I might have done...'

'I'm glad to hear it,' he said with a laugh, 'because I can tell you I was having all sorts of problems with desire on that day, on every day we spent in Italy and on every day since. In fact...' He lowered his voice so that none of the many tourists around them could hear him. 'If I'm honest, I'm having problems with desire at this very moment... seeing you sitting there in the sunlight in that dress and with your hair all wet from the spray...'

'Dominic, you're impossible,' she protested.

'I'm sorry, I can't help it, Mrs Hansford.' He shrugged in true Italian fashion, the gesture exaggerated. 'I guess the only thing for it is to go back to the hotel...it is, after all, almost siesta time.'

'It's at least another hour before siesta,' Claire replied sternly.

'Ah, well,' said Dominic with another helpless shrug. 'What's an hour after all?'

They were staying at the same hotel where they had stayed before, and together they made their way back hand in hand across the sun-dappled piazza and through the narrow streets, totally happy and at ease to be back in that magical city where they had first met and where their love had first unfolded.

It was the sound of a single bell tolling from one of the city's many churches that woke Claire. It was late afternoon and much cooler than it had been earlier. The sun had moved around, filtering through the lower slats of the green shutters covering their bedroom windows, casting golden patterns on the dark wooden floor. A huge fan whirred quietly above the bed with its herb-scented covers of crisp, white cotton edged with deep borders of hand-crafted lace. Turning her head, Claire saw that Dominic still slept at her side, one corner of the sheet wrapped round his naked body, one arm flung protectively across her own body.

They had made love for over an hour until at last, both exhausted but utterly fulfilled, they had slept. Their love-making seemed to get better and better, she reflected, for with every day and week that passed they got to know each other more deeply, discovering untold delights and awakening even deeper passions in each other.

Their wedding day had been wonderful, held in the tiny village church near to her father's and Aunt Marjorie's home, followed by a reception in a local hotel and attended by many of their friends and colleagues from the centre. Melanie and Peter had also been there, much to Claire's and Dominic's delight, and had issued an invitation to their own wedding to be held later in the year.

There had been no hesitation over the choice of honeymoon. 'It has to be Rome,' Dominic said.

'But of course,' she replied. 'Where else would we go?'

Their biggest consideration was where they would live and what they would do once Ben returned to the centre and Dominic's position as locum was at an end. On a temporary basis Claire moved into Dominic's riverside apartment, mainly because it was larger than her flat, but when Dominic talked about looking for a new job she intervened.

'You wanted to go abroad again,' she said one mellow summer's evening as they sat on his balcony and watched the houseboats drift by on the river below.

'Ah, but that was before,' he replied. 'I couldn't go anywhere now and leave you behind.'

'I was thinking I might come with you,' she said slowly.

'Come with me?' The surprise in his voice was apparent

but underlying it she detected an edge of pleasure, excitement almost.

'Would it be possible?' she asked.

'But of course,' he replied eagerly. 'Highly trained nurses are always in great demand.'

'I thought we worked well as a crisis team,' she said, leaning forward to watch one of the houseboats as it slid out of sight behind a curtain of willows. 'Didn't you?'

'Oh, absolutely,' he replied. 'The best.'

And that was how it started. Much discussion followed between the two of them and it was finally decided that they would go abroad to work for one of the children's charities Dominic had previously worked with, initially for a period of two years.

'We may have had enough by then,' Dominic said, 'in which case we will return to England, buy a house, I will seek a partnership in some nice little rural area and if you wish, you could continue with your counselling. And who knows…maybe by then we will be ready to start a family.'

'Sounds wonderful to me,' Claire replied with a little sigh.

Now, as she recalled all the plans they had made, she turned her head again and found that Dominic's eyes were open.

'Hello,' she said softly. 'I didn't know you were awake.'

'I was quite happy just lying here, watching you,' he replied. 'What were you thinking about?'

'Everything,' she replied. 'About the last time we were here, how we met, about the earthquake and all the others, about our wedding day and about all our plans. Do you know, Dominic…' She eased herself onto one elbow and looked down at him. 'Sometimes I still can't believe it all happened. It's like a dream.'

'Well,' he said, looking up at her, 'if it is a dream, I'm in it with you.'

'I know,' she said with a little sigh, 'and it's wonderful, isn't it?'

'Did you know,' he said, 'there's a trip to Assisi tomorrow? Do you think we dare risk it?'

'I don't see why not,' Claire replied. 'In fact, I think we should, seeing we only got to see the hospital last time.'

'So that's tomorrow settled,' said Dominic, 'but what about the rest of today?'

'I don't know,' said Claire. 'Did you have anything in mind?'

'It's funny you should ask that,' said Dominic, moving the arm that was supporting Claire's weight so that she fell across him, 'because, actually, yes, I did have something in mind, very much so.'

'And what is that?' asked Claire, her eyes widening innocently. As Dominic rolled over, imprisoning her beneath him, his intention becoming totally obvious, she lifted her face to his and gave a blissful sigh. 'Oh,' she said, 'silly me, I should have guessed…'